# Wish You Were Here

NATIONAL BESTSELLING AUTHOR

MYUNIQUE C. GREEN

Paperback ISBN: 978-1-105-62762-0

**MyuniqueGreen.com**
**Instagram @ *_cmajor_***

Distributed by iWriteBooks Publishing

*I dedicate this book to my mother, who is very much here, very much part of my life, and continues to shape how I see the world. Her steadiness, care, and sense of humor have carried me through more moments than she probably realizes. This story exists in part because of what I learned from her—about resilience, about showing up, and about choosing warmth even when it would be easier to withdraw.*

# Happy Reading

## CONNECT WITH MYUNIQUE

Amazon

Goodreads

Blog

# The Snowline

The cold arrived in layers.

First through the window seals—a whisper of it, threading past rubber and glass. Then through the vents, metallic and thin. Finally through the door when Amara opened it, stepping onto the platform at Grayhaven Station, and the air hit her face like a fist wrapped in silk.

She'd forgotten how it felt. Not the temperature—she remembered numbers, data points, the clinical language of weather systems. She'd forgotten the weight of it. How it pressed against her sinuses. How her lungs clenched on the first inhale, rejecting the air before her body forced it down.

The train behind her exhaled steam into the falling snow. White on white on white. No horizon. Just snow descending in straight, purposeful lines, as if someone were lowering it on threads.

Amara pulled her scarf tighter and felt the sting in her fingertips even through gloves. Leather-lined, thermal-rated, designed for fieldwork in sub-zero conditions. They'd kept her warm in Nuuk. They felt like tissue paper here.

The platform was empty except for one figure at the far end—a man in a canvas jacket, hood down, dark skin bare to the cold. He stood with his hands in his pockets, relaxed, patient. Watching her.

Tunde.

She raised a hand. He smiled and started toward her, boots crunching through the compressed snow without urgency, without the hunched-shoulder hurry she expected.

"You made it," he said, and pulled her into a hug before she could brace for it. His jacket was cold against her face, but his body radiated warmth. Solid. Unshivering.

"Barely," she muttered into his shoulder.

He laughed and released her, stepping back to get a good look. "You're dressed like you're summiting Everest."

"I'm dressed like a person who doesn't want frostbite."

"It's only twelve below."

"*Only.*"

His grin widened, the kind of grin that said *you'll see.* "Come on. Car's running."

He grabbed her larger suitcase without asking, lifting it like it weighed nothing, and headed toward the parking lot. Amara followed, dragging the second bag over snow that didn't crunch the way snow should. It compressed. It absorbed sound. Her boots left clean impressions that didn't crack or scatter.

The parking lot held a dozen vehicles, all running, exhaust curling upward in pale threads. Tunde's truck sat near the exit—a battered Silverado that had already been old when they were teenagers. Somehow it still ran.

He loaded her bags into the bed, then climbed into the driver's seat. Amara pulled herself up into the passenger side, grateful for the warmth pouring from the vents. She yanked off her gloves and held her hands in front of the heat, fingers aching as blood returned.

Tunde glanced at her, then back at the road as he pulled out onto the main route into town. "How long's it been?"

"Seven years."

"Seven." He said it like he was testing the weight. "You were gone for school, what, four?"

"Four and a half. Then work."

"Greenland, right?"

"Norway first. Then Greenland. Then Chile for a few months."

"Chasing ice."

"Studying ice." She looked out the window. Snow blurred past, unbroken except for the occasional marker post. "Trying to understand what happens when systems collapse."

"Find anything useful?"

"Yeah. They collapse."

He made a sound that might've been a laugh. The heater hummed. Amara's fingers throbbed.

The road curved gently through low hills, trees pressed close on either side—pines and spruces bent under snow but not broken. They looked old. They looked *adapted,* which was the word her brain supplied before she could stop it. She frowned.

"How's the town?" she asked.

"Good. Better than good, actually." Tunde's voice carried something she couldn't name. Pride, maybe. Satisfaction. "We finished the eastern corridor last summer. Full subterranean access from the school to the clinic to the municipal center. No one has to go outside if they don't want to."

Amara turned to look at him. "That's... a lot of infrastructure."

"Took three years. Worth it, though. Especially for the kids."

"Kids shouldn't have to live underground."

"Kids shouldn't have to freeze walking to school." He said it lightly, but there was an edge underneath.

She didn't argue. She was too cold to argue, and her mother's house was still fifteen minutes away.

They passed the town's welcome sign—wooden, carved, dusted with snow that clung to the letters.

**GRAYHAVEN: ESTABLISHED 1893.**

Below it, a newer addition in painted metal:

**POPULATION 1,847.**

Amara stared at the number. "That's up."

"Mm."

"We were at, what, sixteen hundred when I left?"

"About that."

"People are moving *here?*"

Tunde's jaw shifted slightly. "Some. Mostly births."

"Births." She let the word sit. "People are having kids. In this."

"People have kids everywhere."

"Not like this."

"Like what?"

She gestured at the window, the endless white. "This."

"Amara." He said her name carefully. "We're doing fine. I know it looks harsh from the outside, but you'll remember. People adapt."

"People *leave.*"

"Some do."

"Most do."

"Not anymore."

The road widened as they entered the town proper. Buildings appeared—low, compact, roofs heavy with snow. Smoke rose from a few chimneys, thin and gray. Lights glowed in windows, warm and steady. A child in a bright red coat ran across a yard, laughing, no gloves, arms spread like wings.

Amara watched the child disappear behind a house. "How long can a kid play outside here?"

"Depends on the kid."

"Tunde."

He exhaled slowly. "Twenty minutes, maybe thirty if they're moving. Longer if they're born here."

"Longer."

"Yeah."

"Why?"

"I don't know. Better circulation, maybe. Cruz could tell you." He glanced at her. "You'll see it. You'll get used to it again."

"I don't want to get used to it."

"Then you picked the wrong place to come back to."

The words landed harder than she expected. She turned back to the window and watched the town slide past. A woman swept snow from her front steps, methodical, unhurried. A man loaded firewood into a cart, his breath visible but not labored. Everything moved at the same pace—steady, efficient, calm.

Nothing looked wrong.

*That was the problem.*

Tunde slowed as they approached a familiar street. The houses here were older, set farther back from the road, surrounded by bare trees and snow-covered gardens. Amara's chest tightened.

"You good?" Tunde asked.

She nodded.

He turned onto Maple Street and pulled up in front of the third house on the left. Her mother's house.

It looked smaller than she remembered. The blue paint was faded, the shutters slightly crooked, the roof sagging under snow that hadn't been cleared. But the windows were intact. The door was solid. The mailbox still read **OKOYE** in her mother's careful handwriting.

Tunde put the truck in park but didn't turn off the engine. "You want me to come in?"

"No. I'm fine."

"Amara."

"I'm *fine.*"

He studied her for a moment, then nodded. "Spare key's still under the turtle."

"The turtle."

"By the back step. Ceramic thing. Your mom never moved it."

Amara unbuckled her seatbelt and pushed the door open. The cold rushed in immediately, sharper than before. She stepped down into snow that rose past her ankles and pulled her bags from the truck bed. Tunde got out and helped her haul them to the porch.

"I'll check on you tomorrow," he said.

"You don't have to."

"I'm going to."

She managed a thin smile. "Thanks."

He squeezed her shoulder, then jogged back to the truck. She watched him drive away, tail lights fading into the snow, and then she was alone.

The house waited.

Amara climbed the steps—three of them, wood worn smooth under compacted ice. She found the turtle exactly where Tunde said it would be, half-buried beside the mat. The key beneath it was cold enough to burn.

She unlocked the door and stepped inside.

Warmth hit her first.

Unexpected, overwhelming warmth, as if the heat had been trapped inside and concentrated. She closed the door quickly and stood in the entryway, breathing hard, letting her body adjust.

The house smelled like her mother—vanilla, cardamom, old paper. The furniture was exactly as she remembered: the gray couch with its frayed armrest, the bookshelf crammed with mismatched spines, the coffee table her father had built before he died.

But something was wrong.

Amara moved through the living room slowly, her bag forgotten by the door. The thermostat on the wall read seventy-eight degrees. *Seventy-eight.* That was excessive even by her mother's standards.

She walked into the kitchen. A mug sat on the counter, still holding the dark residue of tea. A dish towel hung over the oven handle, neatly folded. The calendar on the wall was turned to February, three weeks out of date.

Her mother had died in February.

Amara touched the mug. It was clean. Someone had washed it and left it there, an artifact of the last morning.

She opened the fridge.

Milk, eggs, vegetables—all expired now, quietly rotting in the cold light. She closed it and leaned against the counter, eyes burning.

The heat pressed down on her. She pulled off her coat, then her sweater, and stood in just a long-sleeved shirt, still too warm. Why had her mother kept it so hot?

She walked to the thermostat and stared at it. The setting was manual, cranked high, the kind of high that would cost a fortune in a town where fuel wasn't cheap.

*Her mother had been cold.*

Amara's throat tightened.

She moved upstairs, each step creaking under her weight. Her old room was at the end of the hall, door half-open. She didn't go in. Instead, she stopped at her mother's room.

The bed was made. The curtains were drawn. On the nightstand sat a glass of water, untouched, and a book—*The Left Hand of Darkness,* a bookmark halfway through.

Her mother had always loved that book.

Amara sat on the edge of the bed and put her face in her hands.

The cold outside pressed against the windows. The heat inside pressed against her skin. And somewhere between the two, her mother had stopped existing.

She didn't cry. She just sat there, feeling the weight of the house, the weight of the town, the weight of seven years that hadn't been long enough.

After a while, she lay down on top of the covers, still dressed, and stared at the ceiling.

The snow kept falling.

The house kept standing.

And Amara, despite everything, fell asleep in the warmth her mother had fought so hard to keep.

# Her Mother's House

Amara woke into a sealed quiet.

Snow packed itself against the house, thick enough to swallow sound before it could travel. The walls held firm, wood tightened by cold, every seam pressed shut. Above her, winter rested with full weight, patient and unmoving. The world felt wrapped, contained, as if the house had been set apart from everything beyond it.She lay still, disoriented, staring at a ceiling she'd last seen as a teenager. The light filtering through the curtains was gray and flat, the kind of light that gave no indication of time.

Her phone said 9:47 a.m.

She'd slept fourteen hours.

Amara sat up slowly, her body heavy and sluggish. The room was still warm—oppressively so. Sweat had dampened her shirt during the night. She peeled it away from her skin and stood, joints protesting.

The house was exactly as she'd left it. Untouched. Waiting.

She walked to the window and pulled back the curtain. Snow covered the yard in a smooth, unbroken sheet. The street beyond was empty. No tire tracks. No footprints. Just snow falling in those same methodical lines, accumulating without drama.

A flicker of movement caught her eye—across the street, a door opened. A woman stepped out in a thin fleece jacket and boots, no hat, no gloves. She walked to the end of her driveway, checked the mailbox, and walked back inside. Thirty seconds, maybe less. Her face had been calm. Not rushed.

Amara's fingers ached just watching.

She let the curtain fall and moved downstairs. The kitchen felt smaller in daylight. The mug on the counter looked more accusing. She opened cabinets until she found coffee—old, probably stale, but it would do.

While the machine sputtered and hissed, she walked through the house properly, taking inventory.

Living room: normal. Books on shelves, photos on the mantel, her father's woodworking tools in a box by the closet.

Dining room: normal. Table set for two, placemats faded but clean.

Bathroom: normal. Towels folded, soap dish empty, shower curtain pulled neatly to one side.

Everything was *maintained.* Her mother had kept the house the way she'd always kept it—orderly, functional, purposeful.

Except for the heat.

Amara returned to the thermostat and stared at it again. Seventy-eight degrees. She pulled out her phone and checked the utility company's website, logging into her mother's account with the password she'd been given by the estate lawyer.

The heating bill for January was four hundred and sixty-three dollars.

February, incomplete, was already at two hundred and ninety.

Amara scrolled back. December: four hundred and twelve. November: three eighty-nine.

She kept scrolling.

Two years ago, January had cost one hundred and forty.

Three years ago: ninety-six.

Her mother had been cranking the heat higher every year. Exponentially higher.

Amara closed the app and pressed her palms against her eyes. *Why?*

The coffee machine beeped. She poured a cup, black, and sat at the kitchen table with her mother's calendar still showing February.

The last entry was the 14th. *Groceries. Call A.*

Call A.

Call Amara.

Her mother had meant to call her. Had written it down, like a reminder, like something she might forget. They'd spoken twice in the months before she died—short, stilted conversations about weather and work. Amara had always meant to call back. There was always something else. A report. A meeting. Another glacier to measure.

She set the mug down harder than she intended.

The doorbell rang.

Amara flinched, then stood and moved to the front door. Through the frosted glass she could see a shape—someone tall, broad-shouldered, holding something.

She opened the door.

Tunde stood on the porch, a casserole dish in his hands, snow dusting his shoulders. He wasn't wearing a coat. Just a flannel shirt and jeans.

"Morning," he said. "You eat yet?"

"Tunde, it's *freezing.*"

"It's fifteen above. Warming up." He stepped inside without waiting for an invitation, bringing cold air with him. "Lila made this. She heard you were back."

Amara closed the door and followed him into the kitchen. He set the dish on the counter and pulled off the foil—some kind of casserole, layered and dense, still steaming faintly.

"She didn't have to do that."

"She wanted to. Everyone does." He glanced at her. "This is a small town. People care."

"People are *nosy.*"

"That too." He smiled, but it faded quickly. "How are you doing? Really."

Amara leaned against the counter and crossed her arms. "I don't know yet."

"You sleep okay?"

"Too well."

"That's the air. It's heavier here. Better sleep."

"It's not better if you don't want to wake up."

Tunde frowned. "Amara—"

"Why was my mother spending five hundred dollars a month on heat?"

He blinked. "What?"

"Her heating bills. I checked. She was running this place hotter than a sauna." Amara gestured around the room. "Why?"

Tunde rubbed the back of his neck. "I don't know. She was... she got cold easy."

"She was fifty-six. She wasn't elderly."

"Some people just run cold."

"Not like this."

He didn't answer immediately. His gaze drifted to the window, then back. "You want to see her?"

Amara's stomach clenched. "See her."

"At the funeral home. Cruz is handling the arrangements, but you're listed as next of kin. You'll need to approve things."

"I thought—" She stopped. "I thought she was already..."

"Prepared, yeah. But not released." Tunde's voice gentled. "You don't have to go today."

"No. I should." Amara pushed off the counter, the motion sharper than she intended. Her palms left a faint chill behind, skin stinging where the laminate had leeched warmth. The room seemed smaller once she stood, ceiling pressing low, corners crowded with everything she had avoided since the call came in.

She grabbed her coat from the chair by the door. The fabric carried the smell of outside—

snow, damp wool, the faint metallic bite that clung to winter air. Sliding her arms into the sleeves felt ceremonial, a signal her body understood before her thoughts caught up. This was movement toward something fixed. Something waiting.

Tunde watched her without speaking. He reached for his keys only after she stepped into her boots, the decision sealed by the scrape of rubber against tile. The door opened with effort. Cold rushed in, sharp and immediate, filling the house as if it had been held back on purpose.

The porch groaned under their weight. Snow shifted and settled, reshaping itself around their steps. Amara pulled her collar higher, breath tightening as the cold claimed her face. The town lay still beyond the yard, buildings half-buried, streets narrowed into pale corridors. Every surface carried the same muted color, as if the world had agreed to keep its voice low.

The car took time to warm. Tunde brushed snow from the windshield in slow, deliberate strokes. Amara stood beside the passenger door, hands clenched in her pockets, watching his breath cloud and vanish. When she climbed inside, the seat felt rigid, unyielding. She folded her hands together and held them there, fingers laced, knuckles pale.

They pulled onto the road. Tires whispered over packed snow. Houses slid past in quiet rows, porches empty, windows dim. The town revealed itself piece by piece—closed shops, a church steeple dulled by frost, the familiar landmarks stripped to shape and outline. Amara tracked each one as it passed, counting distance, bracing herself with motion.

By the time the funeral home came into view, the sky had flattened into a uniform gray. The low brick building waited at the edge of town, narrow windows dark, chimney releasing a thin thread of smoke that rose and thinned into the cold air. Tunde slowed the car. Amara kept her hands folded, eyes forward, breathing measured as the car rolled to a stop.

More people were out now—walking, shoveling, moving between buildings with that same unhurried efficiency. A group of children played in a yard, building something in the snow. One of them—a boy, maybe eight—was bareheaded, his coat unzipped, laughing.

"How long can kids play outside here?" Amara asked again.

Tunde's jaw tightened. "As long as they want."

"That's not an answer."

"It's the only one I have."

They pulled into the funeral home's parking lot. Three other cars sat in the spaces, all running. Tunde turned off the engine but didn't move.

"You want me to come in?"

"No." Amara unbuckled her seatbelt. "I need to do this alone."

"Okay." He reached over and squeezed her hand briefly. "I'll be here."

She stepped out into the cold. It bit immediately—through her coat, through her layers, straight to the bone. She hurried to the entrance and pushed through the heavy wooden door.

Inside, the air was warm and still, scented faintly with something floral and chemical. A woman sat behind a desk near the entrance—older, white, her hair pulled back in a neat bun.

"Can I help you?"

"I'm Amara Okoye. I'm here about my mother."

The woman's expression softened. "Of course. Dr. Cruz is expecting you. Just through that door."

Amara followed the direction she pointed—a hallway leading deeper into the building, doors on either side, all closed. At the end, one stood ajar.

She knocked lightly.

"Come in," a voice called.

Amara pushed the door open and stepped into a small, clinical room. A man stood beside a metal table, his back to her, wearing a white coat over a dark sweater. He turned—Latino, maybe mid-forties, wire-rimmed glasses, tired eyes.

"Ms. Okoye," he said, extending a hand. "I'm Dr. Rafael Cruz."

She shook it. His grip was firm, warm. "Thank you for... for handling this."

"Of course." He gestured to the table. "I want to prepare you. She looks peaceful. No trauma. No distress."

Amara nodded, though her throat felt tight.

Cruz stepped aside.

Her mother lay on the table, the sheet drawn up to her shoulders, its edge straight and deliberate. White against brown skin. Clean. Careful. The room held her in place, every surface arranged around the body as if precision itself were a form of respect.

Amara's gaze moved to her face. Her eyes were closed, lashes resting softly against her cheeks. The lines at the corners of her mouth had eased, leaving behind a calm Amara had rarely seen in life. Her skin held its familiar warmth of tone, untouched by sheen or stiffness. Hair framed her head in the same pulled-back style she wore every day, parted with care, secured with the same quiet discipline she carried into everything.

She looked rested. Composed. As though the strain had finally released its grip.

The air carried a sterile chill, sharp in her lungs, but her focus stayed fixed on that stillness. This was her mother as Amara remembered her in early mornings—eyes closed, breath slow, the world held at a distance. The impulse to speak rose and settled again, caught somewhere behind her ribs.

She stood there, letting the moment stretch, memorizing the exact set of her mouth, the curve of her brow, the way peace had settled into her features as if it had been waiting for permission.

Amara moved closer, her legs unsteady.

"Can I...?"

"Of course."

She reached out and touched her mother's hand where it rested on the sheet. The skin was cool but not frozen. Soft. Her nails were trimmed, clean. There were no signs of struggle. No bruising. No broken capillaries.

"You said exposure," Amara whispered.

"Yes."

"She doesn't look like someone who froze to death."

Cruz was quiet for a moment. Then: "No. She doesn't."

Amara turned to him. "What does that mean?"

"It means the cold here doesn't work the way it does elsewhere." He removed his glasses and cleaned them with the edge of his coat. "Hypothermia typically presents with certain markers—tissue damage, discoloration, cellular breakdown. Your mother has none of those."

"Then how did she die?"

"Her body stopped maintaining heat. Her core temperature dropped below viability. But the process was... gentle."

"*Gentle.*"

"I don't have a better word."

Amara looked back at her mother. "Where did you find her?"

"In her backyard. She was sitting on the bench by the garden."

"Sitting."

"Yes."

"Not collapsed. Not trying to get back inside."

"No."

Amara's hands curled into fists. "That doesn't make sense."

Cruz put his glasses back on. "I know."

"If she was cold enough to die, she would've fought. She would've moved. She wouldn't just *sit there.*"

"Ms. Okoye—"

"Unless she didn't feel it." Amara's voice rose. "Unless the cold didn't register until it was too late."

Cruz said nothing.

"Is that what happened?"

He met her eyes. "I don't know."

"But it's possible."

"Many things are possible."

"That's not an answer."

"No," he agreed quietly. "It's not."

Amara turned back to her mother, her vision blurring. She touched her hand again—cool, still, preserved in a way that felt wrong even if it looked right.

"She kept the house so hot," Amara said. "Did you know that?"

"I visited once. It was warm."

"Seventy-eight degrees. Every day. Why would she do that if she wasn't cold?"

Cruz didn't answer.

Amara stayed there, standing beside the table, her hand on her mother's hand, until the cold inside her chest felt heavier than the cold outside.

Finally, she stepped back.

"I'll approve the arrangements," she said.

"Thank you."

She walked to the door, then stopped. "Dr. Cruz?"

"Yes?"

"Do you think the cold killed her?"

Tunde's words settled between them, heavy enough to bend the air. Amara let them pass through her without catching. She reached for her coat, movements steady, precise, the kind that carried her out of rooms before feeling could gather strength.

The hallway lights blurred into a pale strip as she walked. The door opened. Cold met her face and sharpened her breath. She stepped outside and kept moving, boots finding the path without thought. Gravel shifted. Snow compressed. The world accepted her departure without resistance.

Tunde followed a moment later. He said nothing. He didn't try to close the distance she'd already set.

The drive home unfolded in quiet stretches of road and shadowed houses. Streetlights slid across the windshield in slow intervals, each one marking time she refused to measure. Amara watched the town pass as if it belonged to someone else—storefronts dark, windows dim, roofs burdened by snow that never seemed to thin. Her reflection hovered faintly in the glass, a shape without edges.

The car slowed as they reached the house. Tires crunched, then stilled. The engine clicked as it cooled, a soft mechanical settling that felt final. Tunde turned toward her, his expression careful, expectant.

Amara kept her eyes forward, hands already gathering herself for the walk ahead.

"You okay?"

"No."

"Do you need anything?"

"Answers."

He smiled sadly. "Those are harder to deliver."

She got out, then leaned back in through the open door. "Tunde?"

"Yeah?"

"How many people have died from exposure here in the last five years?"

His expression shifted—something guarded sliding into place. "Why?"

"Just tell me."

"Four."

"Four." She let the number settle. "What's the population again?"

"Eighteen forty-seven."

"That's a low mortality rate for a place this cold."

"We're careful."

"Or you're adapted."

"Amara—"

"I'll see you tomorrow."

She closed the door before he could speak and crossed the yard alone. Snow shifted under her steps, already thinning where her weight passed. The key bit into her fingers when she slid it from her pocket, metal stiff with cold, unwilling to turn until she forced it. The lock gave way with a muted click.

Heat rolled over her as soon as the door opened. It clung to her skin, settled into her clothes, filled the entryway like something that had been waiting. The house held its breath around her. Too warm. Too sealed. Every room carried the same truth it had hours ago. Her mother was gone, and the house knew it.

Amara stood just inside the door, boots dripping onto the mat, snow bleeding into small dark shapes at her feet. The warmth crept higher, up her legs, into her chest, loosening muscles that had stayed tight all day. Her breath slowed. Her shoulders dropped.

Comfort never arrived. Safety stayed out of reach.

Only heat.

It spread anyway, uninvited, settling into her bones as if it belonged there. Amara stayed frozen in the entryway, pulse quickening, the cold already forgotten. That sensation—her body accepting warmth while everything else remained wrong—set a deeper fear in her than winter ever had.

# A New Cold

Amara spent the next morning going through her mother's papers.

Bills. Letters. Medical records that showed nothing unusual—blood pressure slightly elevated, cholesterol within normal range, a prescription for vitamin D that had been refilled monthly. The only anomaly was a note from Dr. Cruz dated six months ago: *Patient reports persistent cold sensitivity. Recommended increased caloric intake and layered clothing. Will monitor.*

Cold sensitivity.

Her mother had *told* someone. And the advice had been to eat more and wear sweaters.

Amara sat back in the desk chair, the paper trembling in her hands. She wanted to be angry, but anger required certainty, and all she had were questions that multiplied faster than she could contain them.

Her phone buzzed. A text from Tunde: *Lunch? I'll come by at noon.*

She glanced at the clock. 11:43. She typed back: *Sure.*

By the time he arrived, she'd moved the papers into neat stacks and opened a window to let some of the oppressive heat escape. The cold air that rushed in felt like relief.

Tunde knocked twice, then let himself in. He carried two paper bags and a thermos, snowflakes melting on his shoulders.

"You're going to freeze this place out," he said, nodding at the open window.

"It's seventy-five degrees in here."

"Exactly. Comfortable." He set the bags on the kitchen table and started unpacking—sandwiches, soup, something wrapped in wax paper that smelled like bread.

"You didn't have to bring food."

"I wanted to. Besides, Lila's casserole won't last forever." He poured soup into two mugs and slid one across to her. "Eat."

She ate.

They sat in silence for a while, the kind of silence that only worked between people who'd known each other long enough not to fill it with noise. Tunde had always been like that—steady, patient, comfortable in stillness.

"You look tired," he said finally.

"I didn't sleep well."

"I thought you said—"

"I *slept.* I didn't sleep well. There's a difference." Amara set down her spoon. "I keep thinking about what Cruz said. About the cold being... gentle."

Tunde's expression tightened. "He shouldn't have said that."

"Why not?"

"Because it makes it sound wrong."

"It *is* wrong."

"No. It's different." He leaned back in his chair. "Amara, your mom... she was struggling. Not just with the cold. With being here. She never adapted the way the rest of us did."

"Adapted how?"

"You know how."

"Say it."

He exhaled slowly. "We're built for this now. Most of us. We don't get frostbite as easy. We don't lose feeling in our fingers after five minutes. Our bodies adjusted."

"That's not adaptation. That's evolution."

"Call it what you want."

"Evolution takes generations, Tunde."

"Then maybe we're lucky."

She stared at him. "You don't actually believe that."

"I believe we're alive. I believe this town works. That's enough."

Amara stood and walked to the window, looking out at the snow-covered street. A woman passed by, pushing a stroller, her breath visible but her pace relaxed. The baby inside was bundled, but the woman wore only a light jacket.

"When did it start?" Amara asked.

"What?"

"The changes. When did people stop feeling the cold the same way?"

Tunde was quiet for a long moment. "I don't know. Gradually. Maybe ten years ago, maybe fifteen. It's hard to pinpoint."

"And no one thought that was strange?"

"People thought it was survival."

She turned to face him. "What do *you* think it is?"

He met her eyes and held them. The steadiness she'd come to expect from him had shifted, settling into something less fixed. His gaze searched and paused, as if he were standing at the edge of a thought he hadn't named yet.

Whatever lived there ran deeper than hesitation. It carried weight. History. The kind of knowing that formed after long endurance rather than sudden shock. His mouth tightened slightly, not from restraint, but from effort—holding something in place that no longer sat easily.

Amara felt it land between them, dense and unspoken. That look stayed with her longer than his words had, pressing into her chest with quiet force, asking nothing and offering no relief.

"I think we're still here," he said quietly. "And a lot of places aren't."

"That's not an answer."

"It's the only one I have."

Amara crossed her arms. "Show me the infrastructure. The tunnels. I want to see what you built."

"Why?"

"Because you're proud of it. And I want to understand why."

He studied her, then nodded. "Okay. This afternoon?"

"Now."

"Amara—"

"Now, Tunde."

He stood and stacked the empty containers with practiced care, lids snapped back into place, edges aligned. The matter was settled the way most things between them were—through action rather than agreement. He set the containers by the door, already moving ahead in his mind, already accounting for what would come next.

They geared up in silence. Amara pulled on her coat, the weight of it familiar, grounding. The boots by the door gave her pause. She flexed her toes inside them, testing the soles, aware of their limits now. Stone and ice demanded more than insulation. They demanded grip. Balance. Endurance.

Outside, the cold met them with clean force. The street lay quiet, snow pushed into orderly banks along the sidewalks, the municipal building rising ahead with its blunt lines and civic indifference. It looked like every other structure meant to endure weather and time without comment. Lights glowed behind a few windows, offices still occupied by people who believed the day's work happened entirely above ground.

They entered through a side door, their footsteps changing as tile replaced snow. The air warmed slightly, carrying the scent of old heating systems and cleaned floors. Fluorescent lights hummed overhead, stretching the hallway into a narrow channel that guided them forward.

At the far end, a door waited apart from the others. No ornament. No warning. Just a metal frame set into concrete, a sign mounted at eye level, its lettering worn smooth by years of passing glances.

EAST CORRIDOR ACCESS.

He reached for the handle without hesitation and swiped a keycard. The door clicked open. Warm air rolled out. "We keep it heated," he explained, gesturing for her to go first. "Not as much as the surface buildings, but enough."

Amara stepped through and found herself at the top of a wide staircase leading down. The walls were concrete, smooth and freshly painted. LED strips ran along the ceiling, casting even white light.

They descended.

The air grew warmer with each step.

At the bottom, the corridor opened into a wide tunnel—tall enough to stand comfortably, wide enough for two people to walk side by side. Doors lined both sides at regular intervals, each labeled:

**STORAGE 3A, MECHANICAL, CLINIC ACCESS, SCHOOL WING.**

"This is the main artery," Tunde said. "Connects the municipal center, the school, the clinic, and the community hall. We're working on extensions to residential areas, but that's slower going."

Amara moved ahead, her boots striking the polished concrete with a sharp, contained sound. She glanced at the walls as she passed, fingertips brushing close without touching.

"Feels wrong down here," she said. "How far under are we?"

"About thirty feet. Depends where you measure from."

"And it's warmer than the street."

"Yeah."

She slowed. "That's consistent all the way down?"

"So far."

She looked over at him. "Explain that."

Tunde kept walking. "We accounted for insulation. Some heat exchange."

"That wouldn't raise the temperature like this. Especially here."

He exhaled through his nose, almost a laugh. "You're assuming we engineered it."

Amara stopped. He took two more steps before noticing.

"You didn't," she said.

"We didn't," he confirmed. "We hit it."

"Hit what."

“The warmth. The deeper we went, the more it climbed. So we adjusted. Reinforced. Kept going.”

“And nobody pushed back?”

“It worked,” he said simply. “People stop asking questions when something works.”

Amara turned to the wall and pressed her palms against the concrete. Heat met her skin immediately—steady, contained, intentional. She pulled her hands back slowly. "Something's wrong," she said.

"Something's working," Tunde corrected. "This town survives because we adapted. Buildings. Systems. Bodies. We didn't fight the cold—we built around it."

"You built *into* it."

"We built *through* it."

She turned to face him. "What happens when it gets colder?"

"It won't."

"How do you know?"

"Because it's been stable for years."

"My mother's heating bills say otherwise."

Tunde's jaw tightened. "Your mother was an outlier."

"Or she was the only one still feeling it correctly."

They stared at each other in the warm, silent tunnel.

Finally, Tunde looked away. "Come on. I'll show you the school wing."

They walked deeper, passing doors and junctions, descending another staircase that led to a second level. Here, the warmth was more pronounced—almost uncomfortable.

"How deep is this level?" Amara asked.

"Fifty feet."

"It's warmer than upstairs."

"Yep."

"That doesn't bother you?"

"Should it?"

They reached a set of double doors marked

**GRAYHAVEN ELEMENTARY**

**LOWER CAMPUS.**

Tunde pushed them open.

Inside, children sat at tables in a wide, open room—reading, drawing, talking quietly. A teacher moved between them, offering guidance. The kids wore light sweaters, some in short sleeves. They looked comfortable. Healthy. Normal.

One of them—a girl, maybe ten—looked up and waved at Tunde. He waved back.

"They do classes down here now?" Amara asked.

"During the coldest months, yeah. Easier than walking outside."

"They shouldn't have to live underground."

"They don't *have* to. They *get* to." He gestured around the room. "Look at them. They're thriving."

Amara watched the children. They moved easily, laughed freely, showed no signs of distress. But something about the scene felt wrong. Not the children themselves—just the fact that they were here, fifty feet below frozen ground, in warmth that shouldn't exist.

"When do they go outside?" she asked.

"Recess. Gym. Whenever they want."

"And they're fine out there?"

"Better than fine."

One of the boys stood and walked toward them—maybe eight years old, dark hair, bright eyes. He stopped in front of Tunde and held up a drawing.

"Mr. Bello, look."

Tunde crouched down to his level. "What've you got, Isaac?"

"I drew the tunnels. See? All the levels." The drawing showed a cross-section of underground corridors, stacked like layers of a cake. At the bottom, the boy had drawn something circular and large, colored in red crayon. "That's the warm part."

Amara's breath caught.

Tunde's smile didn't falter. "That's great, buddy. You're a real architect."

Isaac beamed and ran back to his table.

Amara grabbed Tunde's arm. "What was that?"

"A drawing."

"The red part. At the bottom."

"Kid's imagination."

"Tunde—"

"Not here." His voice was low, firm. He stood and walked toward the exit. Amara followed, her heart pounding.

They climbed back to the main level in silence. When they reached the surface corridor, Tunde stopped and turned to her.

"Kids make things up," he said.

"He drew something specific."

"He drew warmth. That's all."

"You don't believe that."

Tunde's expression hardened. "What do you want me to say, Amara? That there's something weird happening underground? That maybe the town's built on top of something we don't understand? Fine. Maybe it is. But whatever it is, it's keeping us alive."

"Or it's keeping you compliant."

The words hung between them.

Tunde shook his head slowly. "You just got here. You don't understand how things work anymore."

"I understand that my mother's dead and no one seems to care why."

"We *care.* We just accept it."

"That's the problem."

He looked at her for a long moment, something sad and resigned in his eyes. "I'll drive you home."

They didn't speak on the way back.

When Tunde pulled up in front of her mother's house, Amara got out and paused with the door open.

"Thank you," she said quietly. "For showing me."

"Amara—"

"I mean it."

He nodded. "Get some rest."

She closed the door and watched him drive away.

Inside, the house was warm and empty and full of questions she didn't have answers to.

But she knew where to start looking.

Down.

# Moving Target

The clinic sat three blocks from her mother's house—a low brick building with narrow windows and a parking lot that hadn't been plowed in days. Cars sat buried under snow up to their wheel wells. No one seemed to mind.

Amara walked. The cold bit at her exposed skin, sharper today than yesterday, or maybe she was just more aware of it. Her fingers throbbed inside her gloves. Her lungs burned with each breath. By the time she reached the clinic's entrance, her face felt numb.

Inside, warmth enveloped her like a weight.

The waiting room was small and dated—plastic chairs, outdated magazines, a receptionist behind a sliding glass window. Two people sat waiting: an elderly man reading a newspaper, and a woman with a toddler on her lap. The child was barefoot.

Amara stared.

The woman noticed and smiled. "He kicks off his shoes. Can't keep them on him."

"Isn't he cold?"

"Doesn't seem to bother him." She jostled the boy gently. "Do you, sweetheart?"

The toddler giggled and reached for a toy car on the seat beside him.

Amara forced a smile and walked to the reception window. The woman behind it looked up—middle-aged, white, glasses on a beaded chain.

"Can I help you?"

"I'm Amara Okoye. I wanted to speak with Dr. Cruz if he has a moment."

The receptionist's expression softened. "Oh, yes. He mentioned you might stop by. Let me check." She picked up a phone, spoke quietly, then nodded. "He'll be right out."

Amara sat in one of the plastic chairs, her coat dripping melted snow onto the floor. The elderly man glanced at her over his newspaper, nodded politely, and went back to reading. The toddler babbled and played, his bare feet swinging in the air.

The door to the back hallway opened and Dr. Cruz appeared, still in his white coat, a tablet tucked under one arm.

"Ms. Okoye. Come on back."

She followed him down a short hallway into a small office crammed with filing cabinets, a desk, and two mismatched chairs. He gestured for her to sit and closed the door.

"I'm sorry to drop in unannounced," Amara said.

"It's fine. I expected you'd have questions." He sat across from her, setting the tablet on the desk. "How are you managing?"

"I'm not sure yet."

He nodded, as if that were a reasonable answer. "What can I help you with?"

Amara pulled a folded paper from her coat pocket—a printout of her mother's last medical visit. "You saw her six months ago. You noted cold sensitivity and recommended dietary changes."

"I remember."

"That's not a normal recommendation for hypothermia risk."

"She wasn't at risk for hypothermia. Not clinically."

"Then what was she at risk for?"

Cruz removed his glasses and cleaned them slowly. "Misalignment."

"Misalignment."

"Yes."

"With what?"

He put his glasses back on. "With the town."

Amara leaned forward. "What does that mean?"

"It means most people here have adjusted to the climate. Their bodies compensate more efficiently. Your mother's didn't."

"That's not adjustment. That's—"

"Adaptation. I know." He held up a hand. "I'm a physician, Ms. Okoye. I trained in Boston. I know what human physiology is supposed to look like. And I know what I see here doesn't match."

"Then why aren't you reporting it?"

"Reporting it to whom? The state health department? The CDC?" He smiled thinly. "I did, actually. Five years ago. Submitted a full report documenting metabolic variance, cold tolerance markers, cardiovascular efficiency improvements. You know what they said?"

"What?"

"Congratulations on having a healthy population."

Amara sat back. "They didn't investigate?"

"They sent a researcher. She spent three days here, took samples, ran tests. Everything came back normal. Healthy, even. She left and I never heard from her again." Cruz's expression darkened. "The thing is, everyone here *is* healthy. Better than healthy. Lower rates of heart disease, diabetes, respiratory illness. People live longer. Work longer. Recover faster. By every standard metric, this town is thriving."

"Except people are changing."

"Yes."

"And my mother couldn't."

"No." His voice gentled. "She couldn't."

Amara's throat tightened. "Did she know?"

"That she was different? I think so. She never said it outright, but the way she talked... she noticed things. Small things. How other people dressed lighter. Stayed out longer. She asked me once if I thought the town was getting colder or if she was getting weaker."

"What did you tell her?"

"I told her both were possible."

"That's not an answer."

"It's the only honest one I had." Cruz leaned forward, elbows on his knees. "Ms. Okoye—Amara—I don't know what's happening here. I have theories, but no proof. What I *do* know is that something in this environment is facilitating rapid physiological adaptation. Whether it's environmental, biological, or something else entirely, I can't say. But it's real. And it's accelerating."

"Accelerating how?"

"Children born here in the last five years show traits from birth. They don't adapt—they're already adapted. Cold tolerance, efficient circulation, altered sleep cycles. It's not learned. It's innate."

Amara felt cold despite the warm room. "That's not possible in that timeframe."

"I know."

"So, what is it?"

"I don't know."

"Guess."

Cruz was quiet for a long moment. Then: "Something is changing us. Not slowly. Not over generations. *Now.* And the people who can't change..." He trailed off.

"Die," Amara finished.

He didn't argue.

She stood abruptly, needing to move, needing air. "Can I see the records? Birth records, medical histories, anything that shows the progression?"

Cruz hesitated. "They're confidential."

"My mother's dead because of this."

"I know." He stood as well. "Give me a day. I'll pull together what I can without violating ethics protocols."

"Thank you."

She turned to leave, but he spoke again. "Amara?"

She looked back.

"How are you feeling? Physically?"

"Cold. Tired. Normal for being back here."

"Any changes? Faster recovery from exposure? Less pain in your extremities?"

Her stomach dropped. "Why are you asking?"

"Because you've been back three days. And if the pattern holds, you'll start noticing differences soon."

"I'm not staying that long."

"Doesn't matter. The process begins on arrival."

"What process?"

"Adaptation." He said it simply, like a diagnosis. "Everyone who stays begins to change. Some resist longer than others. But eventually..." He gestured vaguely. "You fit, or you don't."

Amara's hands clenched. "I'm not changing."

"I hope you're right."

She left the office, walked through the waiting room without looking at anyone, and pushed out into the cold.

It hit her like a wave, stealing her breath, but she welcomed it. At least out here, the wrongness was obvious. Inside—in the clinic, in the tunnels, in her mother's overheated house—the wrongness wore the mask of comfort.

She started walking, no destination in mind, just moving.

Snow fell in its steady, purposeful lines. The street was quiet except for the sound of her boots crunching through the packed snow. A few houses showed lights in their windows. Smoke rose from chimneys. Everything looked *normal.*

Ahead, a group of children played in a yard—four of them, ages ranging from maybe six to twelve. They were building something in the snow, laughing, shouting instructions to each other. One of the younger ones wore a puffy coat but no gloves, no hat. Another wore only a hoodie.

Amara slowed, watching.

The oldest girl, her hair braided close to her scalp, worked the snow with bare hands, packing it into shape with deliberate care. Her fingers flushed pink against the white, steady as she pressed and smoothed, unbothered by the cold biting into her skin.

"Higher!" one of the younger boys shouted.

"I'm trying," the girl said, laughing. She reached up, placing another layer, her breath visible but her movements easy, efficient.

Amara's own fingers ached just watching.

One of the children noticed her—a boy in the red coat she'd seen yesterday. He waved.

She waved back, uncertain.

He ran over, snow kicking up around his boots. Up close, she could see his face was flushed but not pained. His eyes were bright. Excited.

"Are you Ms. Okoye's daughter?" he asked.

Amara blinked. "Yes. How did you—?"

"My mom told me. She said you used to live here but you left." He studied her with open curiosity. "Are you cold?"

"Yes."

"How come?"

"Because it's freezing."

He tilted his head, considering this. "I'm not cold."

"I can see that."

"Do you want to help us build?" He pointed at the structure in the yard—some kind of fort, walls rising three feet high. "We're making a castle."

"I don't think I can stay outside that long."

"How come?"

"Because I'll get too cold."

He frowned, genuinely confused. "But you're a grown-up. Grown-ups don't get as cold."

"Where I'm from, they do."

"That sounds hard." He said it with such sincere concern that Amara felt something crack in her chest.

"It is," she managed.

"You should stay inside more. It's warmer." He grinned and ran back to his friends, shouting something about turrets.

Amara lingered at the edge of the sidewalk and watched them. Their boots kicked through powder. Laughter cut clean arcs through the air. One of them spun too fast and fell, arms flung wide, then sprang back up with snow clinging to her coat. They bent, scooped, shaped, started over. Their movements carried ease, the kind that came from bodies at home in their surroundings.

Joy moved through them without restraint. It showed in their faces, in the careless way they shed gloves, in the confidence of bare skin meeting winter and continuing anyway. The sight twisted something low in Amara's stomach. Happiness sat easily on them, bright and uncomplicated, untouched by the conditions that framed the scene.

She turned away and headed back toward her mother's house. Cold closed around her as she walked, settling into her cheeks, her hands, her breath. Each step sharpened it. By the time she reached the front door, her face burned dully, fingers stiff and clumsy, lungs aching with every inhale.

The door shut behind her, and warmth rushed in. It clung. It settled fast, curling around her shoulders and down her spine. The shift made her knees buckle. She crossed the room and dropped onto the couch, coat still on, boots dripping onto the floor. Her eyes closed, but the images stayed with her—children laughing, uncovered heads, skin unmarked by frost.

Facts lined up in her mind, insistent and orderly. Bodies reacted to cold. Exposure carried cost. Heat behaved predictably beneath the surface.

The town kept refusing those rules.

Amara opened her eyes, reached for her phone, and pulled up her notes. Her thumbs hovered once, then began to move.

**Observations:**

Population shows extreme cold tolerance

Physiological changes present from birth in recent children

Underground structures warmer than surface

Low mortality rate despite extreme climate

Cold described as "gentle" by medical examiner

Town infrastructure built around descending into warmth

**Questions:**

What is causing the adaptation?

Why is it accelerating?

What happens to those who can't adapt?

What is generating heat underground?

She held her gaze on the last line for a long moment, cursor blinking beneath it, patient. Then she added one more question and let it sit.

What is Grayhaven built on top of?

The phone vibrated almost immediately. The sound cut through the room, sharp against the quiet. An unfamiliar number filled the screen.

*This is Dr. Cruz. I can meet you tomorrow morning. I'll bring what I can. Be careful.*

Amara read the message once. Then again. Her eyes stayed on the final words until they lost their shape and became weight instead.

Be careful.

She set the phone down and let her hand linger beside it, fingers spread as if grounding herself against the table. The house surrounded her, sealed tight, heat pressing from the vents, from the floors, from the walls themselves. It felt overprepared, as if it had been built to hold something at bay rather than welcome anyone inside.

Her mother had lived this way. Careful. Attentive. Always accounting for risk.

That vigilance hadn't saved her.

Amara crossed the room and stopped at the window. Snow drifted down in slow, steady sheets, softening the street into pale shapes. The children were gone now. Only the remains of their work lingered—a half-formed castle slumping at the edges, waiting. It would be there tomorrow. They would come back to it, confident and unguarded, and continue where they left off.

She raised her hand and rested it against the glass.

Heat met her palm.

She pulled back at once, breath catching, pulse surging. The warmth lingered on her skin. It hadn't come from behind the window.

Her eyes dropped to the ground outside, to the snow settling where it shouldn't, to a town behaving as if it answered to a different set of rules. The realization gathered quickly, layering itself without mercy.

The problem wasn't the cold.

It was everything underneath it.

Amara stood there, staring into the falling snow, already certain that tomorrow would pull the town open in ways it hadn't been prepared to withstand. Her phone buzzed again on the coffee table.

She flinched, then exhaled when she saw the screen.

Unknown Number: also, fair warning—Grayhaven mornings run early. If you show up late, I will assume you're dead or ignoring me. Either way, I drink the coffee myself.

A small sound escaped her before she could stop it. Half laugh, half breath. It felt strange in her chest, like a muscle she hadn't stretched in days.

She picked up the phone.

Amara: Duly noted. I'll aim for "alive and punctual."

Three dots appeared almost immediately.

Dr. Cruz: Excellent. Alive is my preferred baseline.

Amara set the phone down, the corner of her mouth still lifted. The house remained too warm. The snow kept falling. Whatever lived under Grayhaven hadn't gone anywhere.

But for the span of a few seconds, the pressure eased.

She moved back toward the kitchen, shrugging out of her coat at last. The kettle waited on the stove, exactly where she'd left it. She filled it, set it down, and turned the burner on. The simple sequence steadied her—water, metal, flame doing exactly what it was meant to do.

As she waited, she leaned against the counter and glanced once more toward the window. The half-built snow castle slumped quietly in the yard across the street, stubborn in its unfinished state.

"Tomorrow," she murmured, more to herself than anything else.

The kettle reached its pitch and cut off with a decisive click. Amara poured the water, watched steam rise and fade, then carried the mug with her to the couch. She sat sideways, feet tucked under her, heat soaking through the ceramic into her palms.

Outside, a single figure crossed the street at an unhurried pace, bundled head to toe, boots leaving shallow impressions that filled in almost as soon as they formed. Someone waved to no one in particular. A porch light flicked on. Ordinary motions stitched the evening together.

Amara took a careful sip. Too hot. She winced and blew across the surface, smiling despite herself. The house creaked softly as the heating system cycled, settling into its familiar rhythm. She let her head rest back against the cushions and stared at the ceiling, tracing a faint crack she'd memorized years ago.

Tomorrow had shape now. A meeting. A place to be. A person who would show up with answers or at least better questions. The thought steadied her more than she expected.

She finished the tea slowly, then set the mug aside and stood. The lights went off one by one as she moved through the house, a quiet ritual she'd inherited without realizing it. At the window, she paused again. Snow continued its patient work, smoothing edges, hiding seams.

"Build all you want," she said under her breath.

Upstairs, she changed, folded her clothes with care, and slid into bed. The sheets were already warm. Sleep came in pieces at first, then settled fully, carrying her into a rest that felt earned.

# Behaving Strangely

The town offices occupied the ground floor of the municipal building—a squat concrete structure that looked like it had been built to withstand a siege. Amara arrived at nine in the morning, her face still numb from the walk, her fingers aching despite two layers of gloves.

The lobby was empty except for a woman behind a desk, elderly, white hair pulled into a bun so tight it looked painful. She looked up as Amara entered, her expression polite but distant.

"Can I help you?"

"I'm Amara Okoye. I'd like to access public records—weather data, historical documents, town planning files."

The woman's expression didn't change. "What time period?"

"Last twenty years."

"That's a lot of material."

"I have time."

The woman studied her for a moment, then stood slowly. "Follow me."

They walked down a narrow hallway lined with closed doors, each labeled with departmental names. At the end, the woman unlocked a door marked **ARCHIVES** and gestured inside.

"Everything's organized by year and category. Weather records are in the blue binders. Planning documents are filed by project date. Historical materials are in the cabinets along the back wall." She handed Amara a key. "Lock up when you're done. Return the key to the front desk."

"Thank you."

The woman left without another word.

Amara stepped into the room and closed the door behind her. The space was small and windowless, lit by flickering fluorescent tubes. Metal shelves lined three walls, packed with binders, file boxes, and rolled documents. The air smelled like old paper and dust.

She started with weather records.

The blue binders were organized chronologically, one per year. She pulled the last five and spread them across the small table in the center of the room.

Each binder contained daily logs: temperature, precipitation, wind speed, barometric pressure. The data was handwritten in neat columns, initialed by whoever had recorded it.

Amara flipped to winter months and started comparing.

**This year - January:** Average high: -8°F. Average low: -18°F. Snowfall: 47 inches.

**Last year - January:** Average high: -7°F. Average low: -17°F. Snowfall: 46 inches.

**Two years ago - January:** Average high: -6°F. Average low: -16°F. Snowfall: 45 inches.

She kept going back.

Five years: -4°F / -14°F / 43 inches.

Ten years: -2°F / -11°F / 38 inches.

Fifteen years: 3°F / -6°F / 31 inches.

Twenty years: 8°F / -2°F / 24 inches.

The progression was smooth. Too smooth. Each year slightly colder, slightly snowier, in increments that felt designed rather than random.

Amara pulled out her phone and opened a spreadsheet, entering the data. Then she graphed it.

The line was nearly perfect—a steady, linear decline with almost no variance.

Natural climate systems didn't work like that. They spiked. They fluctuated. They showed chaos within larger trends.

This looked engineered.

She set the binders aside and moved to the cabinets containing historical documents. Birth records, death certificates, census data. She pulled the files for the last twenty years and started cross-referencing.

**Population:**

Twenty years ago: 1,122
Fifteen years ago: 1,089
Ten years ago: 1,201
Five years ago: 1,544
This year: 1,847

The decline had reversed ten years ago. Not gradually—sharply. And since then, population had grown consistently despite the worsening climate.

She pulled birth records.

Ten years ago: 34 births.

Five years ago: 68 births.

This year: 81 births.

Amara stared at the numbers. Birth rates were *increasing* as conditions worsened. That defied every demographic model she knew.

She opened the death records.

Ten years ago: 52 deaths.

Five years ago: 31 deaths.

This year: 18 deaths.

Mortality was dropping. Significantly.

She checked causes of death. Heart disease, cancer, accidents—all standard. But exposure-related deaths had nearly vanished. Twenty years ago, there were twelve. Ten years ago, eight. Five years ago, three.

This year: one.

Her mother.

Amara's hands trembled as she closed the file.

She moved to planning documents next, pulling folders marked

**INFRASTRUCTURE DEVELOPMENT.**

Project proposals, budget reports, construction timelines.

The subterranean corridor project had begun twelve years ago. Initial plans showed a modest tunnel connecting the municipal building to the school. But amendments had been added year after year, each one expanding the scope, deepening the excavation, extending the network.

She found a geological survey from the early planning stages. The report noted "unexpected thermal readings at depth" and recommended further investigation before proceeding.

A handwritten note in the margin read: *Proceed anyway. Heat is beneficial.*

No signature. No date.

Amara flipped through construction records. Depth measurements for each section:

Municipal access: 30 feet
School wing: 45 feet
Clinic extension: 52 feet
Community hall access: 60 feet

The numbers increased with each expansion, as if the builders were chasing something.

She found a map—a cross-section showing all levels of the tunnel network. Someone had traced the pathways in blue ink, and the pattern was unmistakable: all corridors curved subtly inward, forming concentric rings around a central point beneath the oldest part of Grayhaven.

The town square.

Amara pulled out her phone and took photos of everything—the weather data, the population records, the construction map, the geological survey.

Then she found the photographs.

They were stored in three large boxes labeled

**HISTORICAL SOCIETY - TOWN ARCHIVE.**

Inside: hundreds of photos, some professional, most amateur, spanning decades.

She started with the oldest and worked forward.

**1950s:** People in heavy coats, bundled against moderate cold. Snow visible but manageable. Faces showed discomfort but not distress.

**1970s:** Similar. Coats slightly heavier. Snow deeper. But still recognizably normal winter conditions.

**1990s:** This was where things shifted. Coats were lighter despite heavier snow. People stood outdoors for group photos in conditions that should have required shelter. Faces showed calm. Smiles.

**2000s:** Children playing outside in winter wear that looked insufficient. Adults working outdoors in clothing that wouldn't have been adequate two decades prior.

**2010s:** The difference was stark. People dressed for autumn stood in what looked like arctic conditions. Children in light jackets. Adults in fleece and jeans. Everyone looked comfortable.

**Recent years:** Bare hands. Uncovered heads. Minimal layers. And in every photo—every single one—people looked *happy.*

Amara felt sick.

She was looking at a visual record of human adaptation compressed into decades instead of millennia.

She gathered the photos she'd taken with her phone and began looking for annotations, dates, anything that would explain the discrepancies.

That's when she found the logbook.

It was tucked behind the photo boxes—a simple composition notebook with a black cover, pages yellowed. The handwriting inside was careful, precise, female.

The first entry was dated thirty-seven years ago.

*October 14th. First snowfall of the season arrived three weeks early. Town council attributes this to normal variance. I am not convinced. The cold feels different this year. Purposeful.*

Amara's breath caught. She flipped forward.

*November 8th. Temperatures holding unusually stable. No fluctuation. No warm spells. It is as if something is regulating the cold, maintaining it at a specific threshold.*

*December 2nd. Spoke with Dr. Garrison about physiological changes I've noticed in myself and others. He dismissed my concerns. Said adaptation is natural. But this is not natural. This is not evolution. This is something else.*

*January 19th. The town is building downward. Every new project goes deeper. They say it's for insulation. I think they're being drawn to something.*

*March 5th. Fewer people are leaving. More are staying. It's not loyalty. It's not comfort. They're changing. We're all changing.*

Amara turned pages faster, scanning for critical information.

*June 12th. I've started keeping the house warmer. Not because I'm cold—I don't feel cold the way I used to—but because I need to remember what warmth used to mean. I need to remember that this is not normal.*

*September 30th. My daughter left for college today. I didn't tell her what I suspect. How could I? She thinks I'm paranoid. Maybe I am. But I see the way people move now. The way children are born different. Something is preparing us. The question is: for what?*

The entries continued for years—observations, measurements, desperate attempts to document changes no one else seemed to notice or care about.

The handwriting remained steady until the final entries, where it grew shaky, urgent.

*February 3rd. I am so cold. All the time now. The house is 80 degrees and I'm still cold. Dr. Cruz says my body is rejecting the process. I asked what process. He couldn't answer.*

*February 9th. I think I'm dying. Not from illness. From misalignment. I no longer fit here. The town has moved on without me. My body cannot follow.*

*February 12th. I sat in the garden today. It was peaceful. The cold didn't hurt as much as I thought it would. Maybe that's mercy. Maybe that's just how it ends.*

The last entry was dated February 14th—the day her mother died.

*I think I understand now. We're not being attacked. We're being changed. The question was never whether we would survive. It was whether we would still be human when we did.*

*Amara, if you're reading this: Don't stay. Leave while you still can. The town won't let go easily, but you have to try.*

*I love you. I'm sorry I couldn't explain.*

Amara sat motionless, the notebook shaking lightly between her hands. The pages lay open across her knees, dense with her mother's handwriting—tight lines, margins crowded, dates circled hard enough to bruise the paper. Ink pressed deep, as if force alone could make the words hold.

Her throat tightened. She traced one passage with her thumb, then another, following the rhythm of repetition: measurements taken, observations logged, questions written and rewritten in different words. Weather tables marched down the page in obedient columns.

Temperatures rose where they should have fallen. Ground readings climbed year after year. Beside them, short notes crowded in, clipped and urgent, the handwriting growing sharper as time went on.

A loose photograph slipped free and landed against her coat. She picked it up. Children in winter gear stood ankle-deep in snow, smiling at the camera. No gloves. No hats. Another image showed the same street years later, the same posture, different faces, the same ease. On the back, a date. Then another. And another.

Amara swallowed and turned the page.

Her mother's pen had bitten into the paper here, letters slightly slanted, spacing uneven. The writing carried strain, the kind that came from being heard and ignored. From explaining the same thing too many times. From watching acceptance settle in around her while her own body refused to follow.

Amara closed the notebook with care and slid it into her bag, fingers lingering on the worn cover. The archive room pressed in around her—rows of boxes labeled by year, binders stacked with civic pride, charts that repeated themselves with obedient consistency. Weather that behaved. Numbers that didn't. Faces that changed while conditions stayed fixed.

She stood, shouldered her bag, and took one slow look across the room before turning out the light.

At the front desk, the clerk barely lifted her eyes. "Find what you needed?"

Amara adjusted the strap at her shoulder. "Yes," she said. "Thank you."

The door closed behind her with a muted click. Outside, snow fell in clean, orderly lines, settling without sound. Cold rested over the street, even and complete. Beneath it all, far below the sidewalks and foundations, the ground held its heat, steady and intent, drawing the town inward one quiet degree at a time.

# Beyond the Border

Amara sat in her mother's car—a fifteen-year-old Subaru with rust spots and a heater that wheezed—and stared at the road ahead.

She'd found the keys on a hook by the kitchen door, the car buried under a foot of snow in the driveway. It had taken twenty minutes to dig it out, her hands screaming with cold even through gloves, her breath coming in sharp gasps that hurt her lungs.

But now the engine was running, heat pouring from the vents, and ahead of her stretched the only road leading out of Grayhaven.

She needed to see the edge.

She needed to know if the cold ended where the town ended, or if leaving was even possible.

The streets were quiet. A few people moved between buildings, but no one paid attention to her. She passed the school, the clinic, the municipal building where she'd spent the morning unraveling her mother's final message.

*Don't stay. Leave while you still can.*

Amara gripped the steering wheel tighter.

The road carried her through quiet residential streets before widening into the familiar stretch Tunde had driven days earlier. Houses fell away. Trees closed in. Pines lined both sides, their needles dark beneath layers of snow, branches bowed into practiced arcs that spoke of long adjustment rather than strain.

Amara kept her speed low and her eyes on the dash. The odometer clicked forward with deliberate patience. One mile passed. Then another. Snow continued to fall in straight, disciplined lines, filling the world with a steady downward pull.

Three miles. Four.

At five, something shifted. The snow loosened its formation. Flakes fell with less urgency, their paths beginning to wander. She reached for the wipers out of habit. They moved cleanly across the glass, gliding without drag, leaving the windshield clear with a single pass.

Six miles.

The temperature gauge crept upward. One degree. Then another. Amara's grip tightened on the steering wheel, pulse rising as her eyes flicked between the road and the dashboard.

Seven miles.

The snowfall thinned again. Individual flakes separated themselves, drifting in lazy arcs instead of dropping straight down. The trees reflected the change—snow clung unevenly now, scattered rather than packed, branches lifting slightly as if relieved of weight.

Eight miles.

The sky emptied.

One moment flakes filled her field of view, the next the air stood clear, untouched. The road ahead stretched bare beneath a pale sky, dry in places where snow had never reached. Amara eased her foot off the accelerator and breathed out slowly, aware she had crossed a boundary no sign had marked.

Amara slammed the brakes. The car skidded, tires losing purchase before catching again, coming to rest sideways across the empty road. The engine idled too loudly in the sudden stillness.

She stared through the windshield.

Behind her, snow fell thick and uniform, a solid plane dropping straight from sky to ground, white packed so densely it erased distance. Ahead, the world shifted—bare pavement stretched forward under a flat gray sky, trees standing with only a light dusting clinging to their branches, unchanged and undisturbed.

The divide between the two held sharp and exact.

Amara opened the door and stepped out, leaving the engine running. The air met her with a different pressure. Cold still carried bite, but it moved freely around her, sharp without weight, clean against her lungs. She pulled off one glove and extended her hand.

Nothing touched it.

She took five slow steps forward, boots striking dry asphalt, then turned back. Snow descended twenty feet behind her in a flawless vertical sheet, ending in a straight edge that cut across the road as if drawn there. It reached the ground and went no farther. The surface beneath it stayed bare.

She walked closer, heart thudding, and reached out again.

Snow struck her fingers at once, dissolving against her warmth. She pulled her hand back into clear air, skin dry. Forward again—cold flakes gathered and vanished. Back—nothing. She shifted her stance, one foot planted in snowfall, the other on exposed pavement, her body split between two realities.

A low breath escaped her.

She paced along the divide, matching its curve as it followed the rise and fall of the land. It bent where the road bent, dipped where the ground dipped, holding its shape without wavering. The edge stayed intact, unbroken, disciplined.

Amara reached for her phone and began taking pictures, hands unsteady as she framed the line again and again from different angles. The precision refused to blur no matter where she stood. After the last photo, she swiped to her weather app, eyes narrowing as the screen loaded.

**Current location:** 34°F. Partly cloudy. Wind: 8 mph.

She walked back across the line into the snow.

**Current location:** Signal unavailable.

She crossed back.

**Current location:** 34°F. Partly cloudy.

Crossed into snow again.

**Signal unavailable.**

Her phone struggled before the signal caught, bars flickering as if unsure which side of the line they belonged to. She shifted her weight, one step closer to the clear air, and the screen steadied.

Amara scrolled and tapped Tunde's name.

The ring came through thin and warped, stretched in a way that made her jaw tighten.

"Amara?" His voice arrived dulled, pressed flat at the edges. "Where are you?"

"At the edge," she said. "Eight miles out."

A pause. "The edge of where?"

"The snow. It ends. There's a line. You can stand right up to it and—"

"I know," he said.

Her breath caught. "You know."

"Yeah. Everyone does."

She stared straight ahead, eyes fixed on the clean divide cutting the road in half. "How long."

"Long time," he said. "Ten years. Maybe more."

"Ten years," she repeated.

"We figured it was geographic. Some kind of regional effect."

Her fingers curled around the phone. "This isn't regional."

"I get that it feels wrong—"

"It doesn't feel wrong," she cut in. "It behaves like a barrier."

The word sat between them.

Tunde didn't answer right away. When he did, his voice came softer, careful. "Are you coming back?"

The question landed heavier than the cold. "I'm still looking," she said. "I need to understand what I'm seeing."

"There's nothing to figure out," he replied. "This is just how it works."

"That's not an explanation."

"It's the only one anyone's had." He exhaled. "You've been out there a while. You should head back."

She checked the clock on her screen. "Twenty minutes."

"That's already too long," he said. "Please."

Amara lifted her gaze again, tracing the line where snowfall met open air, where one world yielded cleanly to another. "I'll be back," she said.

She ended the call before he could add anything else.

For a long moment, she stayed where she was, body split by the boundary. One side of her felt the weight of falling snow. The other stood in clear, ordinary cold. The difference pressed against her skin, unmistakable, asking a question the town had learned to stop answering.

Then she walked back to the car, turned it around, and drove toward the boundary.

The snow wall loomed ahead like a physical thing.

She drove through it.

Cold slammed into the car immediately. The temperature gauge dropped—five degrees, ten degrees, fifteen. Snow covered the windshield in seconds, forcing her to turn the wipers to maximum speed.

The world turned white.

Amara drove slowly, following the barely visible road, her hands tight on the wheel. The heater roared, struggling to compensate. Her breath fogged the windows despite the heat pouring from the vents.

Two miles in, her phone buzzed. Signal restored.

A text from Dr. Cruz: *Did you get my message? I have the records. Can you meet tonight?*

She typed back one-handed: *Yes. Where?*

*My house. 447 Oak Street. 8 pm. Come alone.*

Amara pocketed the phone and kept driving.

The snow fell heavier now, pressing down, filling the space around the car. It felt different than it had when Tunde drove her into town. More aggressive. More aware.

Or maybe she was just more aware of it.

Five miles in, she saw the first house. Then another. Then the street opened into familiar territory—residential blocks, then commercial buildings, then the town square with its empty fountain and snow-covered benches.

She parked in front of her mother's house and sat for a moment, engine running, staring at the place her mother had kept so aggressively warm.

*The house is 80 degrees and I'm still cold.*

Her mother had fought it. Had turned up the heat, had documented the changes, had tried to stay herself even as the town transformed around her.

And it had killed her.

Amara turned off the engine and stepped out into the snow. It fell on her face, her shoulders, her exposed hands. Cold, yes. But not as cold as it should have been.

She looked down at her fingers.

They were pink. Not red. Not white.

Just pink.

Her phone hesitated in her hand, signal bars rising and falling as she shifted her stance. One step toward clear air and the screen steadied, brightness locking in as if it had found its footing.

Amara scrolled and tapped Tunde's name.

The ring came through strained, the sound stretched thin before it connected.

"Amara?" His voice carried a slight drag, edges softened, as though it had traveled farther than it should have. "Where are you?"

"At the edge," she said. "Eight miles out."

A brief pause followed. "The edge of what?"

"The snow," she replied. "It ends. There's a line. You can walk right up to it and—"

"I know," he said.

Her grip tightened. "You know."

"Yeah. Everyone does."

She kept her eyes on the road ahead, on the straight divide slicing the world cleanly in two. "How long has this been here?"

"Long time," he said. "Ten years. Maybe more."

"Ten years."

"We chalked it up to geography. Some kind of regional effect."

Her thumb pressed into the side of the phone. "That explanation doesn't hold."

He let out a slow breath. "I get why it unsettles you."

"It behaves like a barrier," she said. The word settled into the space between them, heavy and exact.

Silence stretched on the line.

When he spoke again, his voice had softened, measured. "Are you heading back?"

The question carried weight. More than concern. More than distance.

"I'm still here," she said. "I need to understand what I'm seeing."

"There's nothing to solve," he replied. "This is how the town works."

"That answer doesn't work for me."

"It's all anyone's ever had," he said, then more quietly, "You've been out there a while."

She glanced at the time glowing on her screen. "Twenty minutes."

"That's already too much," he said. "Come back."

Amara lifted her gaze again, following the boundary as it cut across the road, snow falling hard on one side, empty air holding steady on the other. "I'll be back soon," she said.

She ended the call before he could respond.

Amara remained at the edge of the road, boots planted where two versions of the world met. Snow gathered against the left side of her coat, melting and refreezing in quick succession. On her right, the air stayed clean, sharp enough to sting her lungs without weight. Each breath carried a different texture depending on which way she leaned. Her skin registered the divide instantly, nerves lighting up with the effort of holding both sensations at once.

She stepped back at last, fully into clear air, and the snow withdrew behind her as if obeying an unspoken rule. The line held.

By the time she reached her mother's house, dusk had settled into the streets. She shut the door and turned the thermostat up until the numbers climbed past reason. The vents answered at once. Heat flooded the room, heavy and insistent, pressing against her face, her arms, her chest. She stood in the center of the living room and didn't move.

Eighty.
Eighty-five.

The air thickened. Her breath grew shallow. Sweat gathered along her hairline and slid down the back of her neck. Her shirt clung. The house creaked softly as it adjusted, working harder, sealing itself tighter.

She stayed there and let it overwhelm her.

This was what too much felt like. This was the edge her body pushed back against. She held onto it until the discomfort sharpened, until her pulse thudded loudly in her ears, until her skin flushed and her legs threatened to give.

Her mother had stood here. Day after day. Letting heat remind her of where the line used to be.

Amara turned the thermostat down and collapsed onto the couch, hands trembling, breath uneven. The room cooled slowly, reluctantly, as if resisting the change.

Outside, snow continued its steady descent, piling where it always did.

Inside, the house stayed alert, holding warmth close, guarding against a cold that pressed from every side.

Amara reached into her bag and pulled out the notebook. The cover bent easily in her hands, softened by years of use. She opened to the final page and read the last entry again, her mother's handwriting tight and urgent.

Don't stay. Leave while you still can.

She checked the clock. Eight hours until morning. Eight hours until Cruz arrived with whatever pieces he was willing to share.

Amara closed the notebook and rested it against her chest. The snow outside thickened, flakes stacking faster now, filling the dark with motion. She watched it through the window, aware of the invisible line miles away, aware of the one she had already crossed.

The question settled into her, heavy and unavoidable.

Whether the boundary existed to protect the town from what lay beyond it—or to protect the rest of the world from what Grayhaven was becoming.

The thought tightened in her chest until it demanded motion.

Amara pushed off the couch and paced the length of the living room. The floor was warm beneath her feet, heat rising through the soles of her socks as if the house itself resisted being ignored. She stopped at the window again, fingers curling against the sill, eyes tracking the snowfall as it erased the streetlight's reach inch by inch.

Protection implied intent.

Containment implied decision.

Her jaw set. She crossed to the thermostat and stared at it, thumb hovering, then turned it down another degree. The vents responded with a faint lag, air shifting reluctantly, as though the house disagreed. She laughed once under her breath, sharp and humorless.

"Yeah," she said aloud to the empty room. "I noticed."

She moved through the house with purpose now, opening doors, checking rooms she already knew by heart. Her mother's bedroom. The spare room. The bathroom with the cracked tile that never stayed cold. Everywhere, the same stubborn warmth. Everywhere, the same quiet insistence.

She stopped in the hallway, palms braced against the wall. Heat pressed back through the plaster. Solid. Steady.

"You don't get to decide," she said, voice tight. The words landed and stayed, absorbed without answer.

Anger rose then, clean and focused. Not panic. Not fear. A sharp refusal to accept what the town had settled into so easily. To accept the way everyone had adjusted their bodies and expectations and language until the impossible became routine.

Her mother hadn't adjusted.

Amara straightened and went back to the couch, grabbing her bag and pulling the notebook free again. Pages flipped faster this time, paper whispering softly as dates and diagrams blurred past. She stopped at a section marked with folded corners, breath coming quicker as she scanned.

"Okay," she said, the word steady despite the pulse in her throat. "Fine."

The words lingered in the air longer than she expected.

Amara snorted softly and shook her head. "Listen to you," she muttered, then caught herself and laughed again, quieter this time. Talking to an empty house. Arguing with the walls. Her mother would have raised an eyebrow at that.

She could hear it anyway, clear as if it had been spoken aloud.

*Nwa m,* said in that dry, unimpressed tone. *If you're going to talk to yourself, at least wait until you have proof.*

Amara pressed her lips together, the smile tugging despite everything. "You always said that," she replied automatically, then winced and laughed again. "See? Still doing it."

She sat back and rubbed a hand over her face, heat clinging to her skin, pulse still running fast. The laugh drained off, leaving behind something sharper, more focused. Her mother's voice didn't soothe her. It centered her.

Proof. Always proof.

Amara leaned forward again, notebook balanced on her knees, pen tapping once against the margin. Diagrams. Measurements. Times. Locations. Her mother hadn't speculated. She'd recorded. She'd tested. She'd returned to the same questions from different angles, stubborn as winter itself.

"That's the part they missed," Amara said, softer now. "You weren't guessing."

Outside, snow continued to stack against the glass, flakes blurring together into a solid white field. Inside, the house held its warmth with quiet determination. Between the two, Amara sat steady, laughter gone, resolve settling in its place.

# Underground

Dr. Cruz's house sat on Oak Street, a narrow residential road where the houses leaned close together as if seeking warmth from one another. Amara arrived at 7:58 pm, her breath clouding in the cold, her hands already aching despite the short walk from where she'd parked.

The porch light was on. She knocked twice.

Cruz opened the door immediately, as if he'd been waiting just inside. "Come in. Quickly."

She stepped into a small, cluttered entryway. The house was warm but not oppressive—maybe seventy degrees, comfortable by anyone's standards. Cruz closed the door and locked it, then gestured toward the kitchen.

"Coffee?"

"Please."

She followed him into a kitchen that looked lived-in: dishes in the sink, papers spread across the table, a cat curled on a chair. Cruz poured two mugs from a pot that looked like it had been sitting for hours. He handed her one and sat down, pushing aside some of the papers.

"I pulled what I could without raising flags," he said, tapping a manila folder. "Birth records, medical histories, developmental charts. It's all anonymized, but you'll see the patterns."

Amara sat and opened the folder.

The first document was a chart tracking developmental milestones for children born in Grayhaven over the last fifteen years. Normal markers—walking, talking, fine motor skills—were consistent with national averages. But there were additional categories she'd never seen before:

**Cold tolerance (unprotected exposure time)**

**Core temperature stability**

**Peripheral circulation recovery**

**Thermal regulation efficiency**

For children born fifteen years ago, the numbers were close to baseline. But with each subsequent year, the metrics improved. Children born five years ago showed double the cold tolerance. Children born this year showed triple.

"They're not adapting," Amara said quietly. "They're being born different."

"Yes." Cruz leaned back in his chair. "I've been tracking this for eight years. At first, I thought it was selection bias—healthier families choosing to stay, weaker ones leaving. But the data doesn't support that. This is direct physiological change, expressed in newborns."

"That's not possible without genetic modification."

"I know."

"So what's modifying them?"

Cruz took off his glasses and rubbed his eyes. "I don't know. I've run every test I can think of. Blood work, genetic screening, environmental analysis. Nothing shows up as abnormal. Whatever's causing this, it's either operating below our detection threshold or it's something we don't have the tools to identify."

Amara flipped through more documents. Growth charts showed children developing slightly faster than national averages. Cardiovascular efficiency was universally high. Immune responses were robust. By every conventional measure, the children of Grayhaven were *thriving.*

Except they weren't quite human anymore.

Or maybe they were *more* human. More fit for the world they were inheriting.

"What about adults?" Amara asked. "Are we changing too?"

"Yes. But slower. Your generation—people who grew up here before the changes accelerated—show moderate adaptation. People who arrived as adults adapt even more slowly. Some never do."

"Like my mother."

"Like your mother."

Amara set down her mug. "I need to see it. The source. Whatever's under the town."

Cruz's expression shifted—something wary sliding into place. "What makes you think there's something under the town?"

"Isaac Reed's drawing. The construction maps showing concentric patterns. The fact that warmth increases with depth. The geological survey that mentioned 'unexpected thermal readings' and was ignored." She met his eyes. "You know there's something down there. You've known for years."

He was quiet for a long moment. Then: "I've suspected."

"Have you looked?"

"No."

"Why not?"

"Because I'm afraid of what I'll find." He said it simply, honestly. "And because I'm afraid that once I know for certain, I'll have to make choices I'm not ready to make."

"What kind of choices?"

"Whether to protect the town or warn the world. Whether to save the people who've already adapted or stop the process before more are changed. Whether I'm witnessing evolution or infection." He put his glasses back on. "Those aren't medical questions, Amara. They're moral ones. And I don't have answers."

"I need to go down there."

"Alone?"

"If necessary."

Cruz stood and walked to the window, looking out at the snow-covered street. "There's a maintenance shaft beneath the municipal building. Older than the tunnels Tunde showed you. It was sealed off ten years ago, marked as structurally unsound. But I know where the access panel is."

"How do you know?"

"Because I tried to open it once. Four years ago. I got as far as the first seal before I turned back." He turned to face her. "I felt it, Amara. The warmth. It wasn't ambient heat. It was *active.* Like standing near something alive."

"Did you tell anyone?"

"I told Tunde. He said the shaft was dangerous and I should leave it alone. He wasn't wrong."

"But you kept thinking about it."

"Every day."

Amara stood. "Take me there. Now."

Cruz hesitated. "It's almost night."

"So?"

"Things feel different at night. Quieter. Like the town is sleeping."

"Is that when it's most active?"

Cruz's silence stretched just long enough to harden her resolve. Amara held his gaze, shoulders squared, already shifting her weight toward the door. The decision had settled. She felt it lock into place somewhere deep and unmovable.

"I'm going," she said. "With or without you."

Cruz drew a breath through his nose, slow and measured. The tension left his shoulders in a controlled release. He nodded once, as if conceding to a familiar argument rather than a new danger.

"Five minutes," he said. "I'll grab a flashlight."

Amara waited while he moved through the back rooms, cabinets opening and closing, metal clinking softly against metal. The building carried sound differently at this hour. Each footstep lingered, echoing off concrete and tile, amplified by the absence of voices. Fluorescent lights buzzed faintly overhead, their glow stripped down to emergency strips that cast long, uneven shadows along the walls.

When Cruz returned, flashlight in hand, he didn't meet her eyes. He checked the batteries instead, thumb pressing the switch twice, beam flaring bright and steady.

They stepped outside together. The cold met them immediately, sharper here where the town thinned and the buildings stood farther apart. The municipal structure loomed ahead, squat and practical, its windows dark, its brick face damp with melting snow. No sign marked it as anything more than offices and records and permits. The kind of place designed to disappear into routine.

Cruz unlocked a side entrance. The door opened with a muted groan, releasing a breath of stale indoor air that smelled faintly of cleaning solution and old paper. Inside, the corridors lay stripped of their daytime identity. Emergency lights traced the floor at knee height, casting the halls into bands of amber and shadow. Every surface reflected a dull sheen, polished for use rather than beauty.

Cruz closed the door behind them and slid the lock home. The sound rang louder than it should have.

“I’m on the volunteer safety committee,” he said as they started down the hall. “Gives me access after hours.”

Amara nodded, eyes tracking the way the corridor narrowed ahead, how the light thinned as they moved deeper into the building. The air felt different here—cooler, heavier, carrying the faint scent of earth beneath the institutional layers.

They moved through empty hallways, their footsteps echoing on tile floors. The building felt different at night—not menacing, but expectant. Waiting.

Cruz led her to a stairwell marked **BASEMENT ACCESS - AUTHORIZED PERSONNEL ONLY.** They descended two flights into a space that smelled of concrete and stale air.

The basement was a maze of storage rooms, mechanical systems, and abandoned equipment. Cruz navigated with practiced ease, weaving between shelves and ducking under low pipes, until they reached a dead end.

A metal panel covered part of the wall, secured with bolts and marked with faded warning signs: **STRUCTURAL HAZARD. DO NOT ENTER.**

"Here," Cruz said.

Amara ran her hand over the panel. It was warm.

Not hot. Not feverish. Just warm, like skin.

"Help me open it."

Together they pried the bolts loose—years of rust had fused some of them, but the metal beneath was oddly clean, as if something had preserved it. The panel came free with a groan.

Behind it: darkness. And a narrow shaft descending into the earth, metal rungs set into the concrete wall.

Warm air rolled upward, carrying a smell Amara couldn't identify—organic but not rotten, mineral but not chemical. Complex. *Alive.*

Cruz aimed his flashlight down. The beam penetrated maybe thirty feet before being swallowed by the dark.

"We don't have to do this," he said quietly.

"Yes, we do."

Amara swung herself into the shaft and started climbing down. The rungs were warm under her hands. After a moment's hesitation, Cruz followed.

They descended in silence, the only sound their breathing and the faint scrape of boots on metal. The air grew warmer with each rung. Amara's coat became oppressive. She paused to unzip it, one-handed, clinging to the ladder with the other.

"How deep does this go?" she called up to Cruz.

"I don't know. I only made it to the first landing."

"How far down is that?"

"Sixty feet, maybe."

Amara kept climbing. Her legs burned. Her hands were slick with sweat. The warmth pressed against her skin like something physical, like the air itself had weight.

Then her foot found solid ground.

She stepped off the ladder onto a concrete platform, Cruz dropping down beside her a moment later. His flashlight swept the space—a circular chamber, maybe fifteen feet across, with three corridors branching off in different directions.

The walls were smooth, too smooth for hand-poured concrete. And they were warm to the touch.

"Which way?" Amara asked.

Cruz pointed to the central corridor. "That one slopes deeper."

They walked.

The corridor pinched tight around them, shoulders brushing stone on either side. The ceiling pressed low enough that Amara had to angle her spine forward, neck bent, breath shortened by posture alone. Moist air clung to her skin, heavy and warm, filling her lungs with each inhale. It carried a faint mineral tang beneath the damp, something older than pipes or walls. Sweat gathered quickly along her spine, her shirt sticking as if the tunnel had reached out and claimed it.

Their steps landed softly, swallowed almost immediately. The floor sloped downward in a gradual curl, turning them in a slow spiral that drew them deeper with patient insistence. The curve felt deliberate, shaped by purpose rather than utility. Each turn tightened her awareness, a sense of being guided rather than led.

After several dozen feet, the passage widened without warning.

Cruz stopped short. Amara barely caught herself before colliding with his back.

"Oh god," he said, the words stripped thin by awe and fear.

The flashlight beam swept forward and caught the walls.

They rose in layered arcs, ridged and striated, their surfaces catching light in soft gradients of pale ivory deepening into ochre. Lines ran through them in repeating bands, close together, each one marking a stage of formation. The texture held a strange balance—smooth beneath the eye, firm beneath suggestion, as if pressure alone had taught it how to exist. The chamber curved inward and up, enclosing them in a space that felt assembled rather than built.

Amara stepped past Cruz, drawn forward without thinking. The air here felt warmer still, carrying a faint vibration she sensed more than heard. She lifted her hand and pressed her palm against the wall.

Heat met her immediately.

The surface yielded just enough to register contact, solid but responsive, holding warmth in a way that felt intentional. Her breath caught. She left her hand there, skin tingling, aware with sudden clarity that this place had not been shaped by tools or plans.

The warmth held steady beneath her palm. Beneath that, a subtle rhythm answered her touch—pressure rising, easing, repeating with patient consistency.

Amara recoiled, breath catching as she pulled her hand back to her chest.

"It's pulsing," she said, voice tight.

Cruz swallowed hard. "It's been doing that for as long as I've known about it."

The flashlight beam wavered between them, skimming over curved walls that followed no human blueprint. The chamber enclosed them completely, a space shaped by accumulation rather than assembly. Every surface carried the same quiet intent.

"How far does this go?" Amara asked.

Cruz shook his head once. "No one's ever found the bottom."

Her jaw set. "Then we keep moving."

"Amara—"

"We don't turn back now."

He studied her face, the heat painting his skin with a dull sheen. After a moment, he nodded.

They continued downward.

The passages shifted as they descended. Straight lines softened. Corners rounded into gradual turns. The air thickened further, clinging to her throat and skin. Heat gathered fast now, building with every step. Amara tugged off her coat and draped it over her arm. Minutes later, her sweater followed. Sweat traced a slow path down her spine, dampening her shirt, darkening the fabric at her collar.

Distance lost meaning. Her legs burned. Her pulse stayed elevated. She tried to count steps, then abandoned the effort.

The corridor widened again.

They emerged into a space so vast the flashlight couldn't claim its edges. The ceiling arched high overhead, layered in broad, ribbed curves that drew the eye upward and failed to meet. The floor beneath their boots felt smooth and faintly responsive, giving just enough to register their weight.

Cruz swept the beam across the chamber.

In its center rose a massive column, rooted deep below and extending upward beyond sight. Its surface carried dense patterns—rings, channels, branching lines that spread and rejoined in deliberate paths. Color moved across it in slow transitions, cream deepening into amber, amber darkening toward red, then easing back again.

The structure expanded and settled in a steady cycle. With each motion, warmth rolled outward, pressing against Amara's skin in soft waves. The air responded, shifting temperature with the rhythm, thickening and loosening in time.

She stood still, chest tight, every sense overwhelmed by scale and presence.

This was what the town rested upon.

This was what fed the heat, shaped the snow, drew the boundaries no one questioned.

Amara felt a sharp, steady anger take hold—not fear, not wonder, but something clean and unyielding.

"What have you done," she said quietly, unsure whether she was speaking to Cruz, the town above them, or the thing itself.

Amara stepped closer, transfixed.

"Don't touch it," Cruz warned.

She stopped three feet away. This close, she could see finer details—smaller structures embedded in the larger mass, thread-like connections that disappeared into the surrounding rock, patterns that repeated at different scales.

It was beautiful.

It was monstrous.

It was *waiting.*

"What is it?" she whispered.

"I don't know." Cruz's voice was small in the massive space. "Nothing from Earth. Or maybe something that was here long before us."

"How long has it been here?"

"I don't know that either."

Amara reached out, not quite touching, feeling the heat radiate from the surface. Her hand trembled.

"It's changing us," she said. "All of us. The children. The adults. The whole town. This is what my mother was fighting."

"Yes."

"And if we destroy it?"

Cruz was quiet for a moment. "Everyone who's already adapted dies. Their bodies can't regulate temperature without it anymore. They're symbiotic now."

"And if we don't?"

"It keeps spreading. Keeps changing more people. Keeps preparing us for whatever it's preparing us for."

Amara pulled her hand back. "We have to tell someone."

"Tell them what? That there's an alien organism under the town? That it's terraforming humans instead of planets? That we're either victims or the next stage of evolution and we don't know which?"

"Yes. Exactly that."

"They won't believe you. They didn't believe the state researcher. They didn't believe your mother. They won't believe you."

"Then I'll bring proof."

“What proof?” Cruz said, his voice tight as he swept his arm across the chamber. “This?” The beam of the flashlight shook as it traced the towering column. “No one comes down here to help. They come to claim it. To catalog it. To turn it into leverage. However it ends, Grayhaven doesn’t survive.”

Amara didn’t answer. She stood rooted to the spot, heat washing over her in steady waves, skin prickling as the structure continued its slow internal cycle. Each expansion pressed outward through the air, through the floor, through her chest. The scale of it settled into her bones at last. Not wonder. Not disbelief. Weight.

Every choice carried consequence. Every path led somewhere final.

She drew a breath that tasted thick and mineral-heavy. "I need to leave," she said, the words coming fast, sharp with urgency. "Right now."

Cruz didn't argue. He turned and started back the way they'd come.

The climb felt longer than the descent. Heat clung harder now, wrapping around her throat, her spine, her temples. The passages seemed narrower, the curves tighter, as if the space resisted release. Sweat soaked her shirt completely. Her legs trembled with effort. Time lost coherence, measured only by breath and step and the growing ache in her muscles.

When they finally broke through into the basement, light struck her eyes too bright, too flat. Ninety minutes had passed. It felt like more.

Cruz sealed the panel behind them with deliberate care, sliding metal into place, fastening locks one by one. The sound rang sharp in the enclosed space.

Outside, cold crashed into her with clean force. Amara staggered a step into the parking lot and tilted her face upward, snow landing against her skin, sharp and grounding. She stood there and let it strip heat from her, let it burn and sting and remind her of limits.

The relief lasted only seconds.

Beneath the pavement, beneath the concrete and pipes and foundations, warmth persisted. Steady. Unmoved by distance. She felt it through the soles of her boots, faint but unmistakable.

The thing below continued its work.

Heat moved upward in slow increments, diffused through layers of earth and stone, softened just enough to pass as natural by the time it reached the surface. Streets above absorbed it without question. Pipes adjusted. Foundations held. The town had been shaped around that steady output—homes built closer together, insulation doubled, heating systems oversized and always running a little hotter than necessary. No one called it excess. They called it comfort.

Amara stood still and let the snow settle on her coat. Around her, the municipal lot lay quiet, its lamps casting dull halos through the snowfall. The building behind her looked ordinary again, brick and glass and locked doors, giving away nothing of what lay beneath. That was part of it too—the way Grayhaven learned to look harmless.

She could see the patterns now. The way winter festivals stretched longer here than anywhere else. The way kids played outside past dusk without gloves. The way no one ever complained about heating costs, even when fuel prices rose everywhere else. How the town shrank slowly, not from loss but from reluctance—people leaving and never quite explaining why, newcomers arriving and settling fast, as if something eased them into place.

Adaptation masquerading as tradition.

Cruz stood a few feet away, shoulders hunched, arms wrapped tight around himself. He didn't look at her. He didn't need to. They were both standing on the same truth now.

"This is why the line holds," Amara said quietly. "The snow. The boundary. It's regulating."

Cruz nodded once. "Keeps the heat contained. Keeps attention away."

"And the town stays intact," she said. "As long as nothing disrupts it."

"As long as nobody digs too deep," he replied.

Her gaze drifted to the street beyond the lot, to the faint glow of houses tucked beneath falling snow. Somewhere under those roofs, people slept easily, bodies warm, unaware of the balance being maintained beneath them. Somewhere, children would wake tomorrow and finish building a half-formed castle, bareheaded and laughing, trusting the ground to hold.

Amara exhaled slowly. The anger she'd felt underground hadn't faded. It had clarified.

Grayhaven wasn't cursed. It was sustained.

And sustenance always came from somewhere.

She turned away from the building and started toward her car, already thinking in steps and timelines. Eight hours until morning had felt generous before. Now it felt dangerously small.

# The Greenhouses

Amara didn't sleep.

She lay in her mother's bed, staring at the ceiling, feeling the warmth of the house press against her skin. But underneath that warmth—underneath the floors, the foundation, the frozen earth—she felt something else.

The organism. Waiting. Breathing. Changing them all.

At 6 am, she gave up and went downstairs. Made coffee. Sat at the kitchen table with her mother's notebook open in front of her.

*We're not being attacked. We're being changed.*

Her phone buzzed. A text from Tunde: *Lila wants to show you the greenhouses. Says you were asking about agriculture. 9 am?*

Amara stared at the message. Part of her wanted to refuse, to pack whatever she could carry and drive straight through the snowline, consequences be damned.

But understanding demanded range, not just proximity. One chamber, one boundary, one buried structure wasn't enough. She needed to trace the reach of it—how far the warmth traveled, what it fed, what depended on it without ever naming the source.

Her phone rested warm in her palm as she reread Cruz's message. A meeting was a start, but starts could mislead. Infrastructure told the truth more reliably than people.

She typed back: I'll be there.

The reply came almost immediately. A simple acknowledgment. A location pin. No reassurance.

Amara pocketed the phone and moved with purpose. Keys. Coat. Boots. The door closed behind her with a final, solid sound. Outside, the street absorbed her departure without comment, snow swallowing her footprints as quickly as they formed. She drove slowly, letting familiarity reassert itself—rows of houses softened by white, streetlights dulled to halos, the quiet competence of a town that functioned smoothly even under constant winter.

The road toward the outskirts opened wider, traffic thinning to nothing. Utility lines traced neat paths overhead. Fences appeared, then stretches of open land shaped by careful use rather than neglect. The air felt different here—still cold, but looser, carrying faint hints of damp earth beneath the snow.

The greenhouses rose ahead in a low cluster, glass roofs slanted to shed accumulation, metal frames locked together in repeating angles. From a distance, they looked unassuming. Practical. The kind of operation meant to serve a town without drawing attention. A few vehicles sat parked along the perimeter, their tires half-buried, engines long cooled.

Light glowed from within the structures, soft and diffuse, casting a muted green through the frosted panels. Steam gathered along the seams where glass met frame, escaping in thin trails that vanished quickly into the cold air.

Amara slowed and pulled in, cutting the engine. The sudden quiet pressed close. She sat for a moment, eyes fixed on the glow ahead, aware that whatever lived beneath Grayhaven had found ways to surface far beyond the municipal building.

If she wanted to understand the scope, this was where it would start.

Lila met her at the entrance and immediately led her to a stairwell. "The real work happens below," she explained, descending. "Surface greenhouses are just for show. Proof of concept. The actual food production is down here."

They emerged into a vast underground space.

It was *enormous.* Easily the size of several football fields, the ceiling supported by concrete pillars, lights hanging in rows that mimicked sunlight. And everywhere—*everywhere*—plants grew.

Row after row of raised beds and vertical towers, dense with leafy greens, fruiting vegetables, grain stalks heavy with seed. The air was humid and warm, thick with the smell of soil and growth.

"This is impossible," Amara breathed.

Lila laughed, delighted. "That's what everyone says. Come on."

She led Amara between rows of tomato plants, each one laden with red fruit. Workers moved through the space—maybe a dozen people, checking plants, harvesting, adjusting irrigation lines. They wore light clothing: T-shirts, cargo pants, boots. Several were barefoot.

"How deep are we?" Amara asked.

"Seventy feet. Deeper in the back sections—some go to ninety."

"And the temperature?"

"Varies by zone. Here it's about seventy-five. In the germination rooms, we keep it closer to eighty." Lila stopped at a bed of leafy greens and ran her hand over the leaves with obvious pride. "Kale. Swiss chard. Collards. Year-round production. No seasonality."

"How?"

"Soil." Lila crouched and scooped up a handful, letting it fall through her fingers. "Look at this. Perfect texture. Rich nutrients. And warm. Always warm."

Amara knelt and touched the soil.

It was warm. Not from heat lamps or artificial systems. *Warm.*

"Where does the warmth come from?"

"Geothermal, we think. Maybe underground water systems. Tunde did a survey years ago but couldn't pinpoint the source." Lila stood and brushed off her hands. "Honestly, we stopped asking. It works. That's what matters."

"It works because something is generating heat."

"Yes. The earth."

"Lila, the earth doesn't work like that. Not here. Not at this depth."

Lila's smile didn't falter, but something shifted in her eyes. "Then I guess we're lucky."

Amara stood. "Can I see the deeper sections?"

"Sure. But it's warmer down there. You might want to leave your coat."

Amara hadn't brought a coat. She was already too warm.

They walked through the growing zones, past beds of root vegetables and fruiting vines, past workers who waved cheerfully at Lila. Everyone looked healthy. Content. *Adapted.*

At the far end of the corridor, the space narrowed again, funneling them toward another stairwell. Warm air drifted up from below, heavier with each step down, carrying the smell of soil and leaves and something faintly sweet.

"This section's the newest," Lila said over her shoulder as they descended. "Opened last year. We started pushing boundaries a little more down here."

Amara wiped her palms on her jeans. The heat settled fast, spreading across her back, gathering at the base of her neck. "Pushing how."

"By growing things we were never supposed to grow." Lila smiled, casual, proud. "Citrus. Peppers. Melons. Stuff that hates winter."

The lower level opened wide, and Amara slowed without meaning to. The air wrapped around her, damp and warm enough to fog her breath. Rows of plants stretched out in dense, layered greens, leaves broad and glossy, vines spilling over the edges of raised beds. A lemon tree stood near the walkway, branches sagging under the weight of fruit, yellow bright against the foliage. Pepper plants crowded one another, heavy with color. Thin vines climbed their supports and curled back on themselves, dotted with small green melons still gaining size.

Her skin prickled.

"This is insane," Amara said quietly.

Lila laughed. "This is productive." She reached up, twisted a lemon free, and held it out. "Here. Try it."

Amara hesitated, then took it. The peel split easily under her fingers, releasing a sharp citrus scent that cut through the humidity. Juice slicked her hands as she pulled the segments apart. She bit down.

The flavor hit full and immediate—bright, sweet, sharp in a way that made her mouth water. Juice ran down her wrist before she noticed.

She stared at the fruit. "This is… ridiculous."

Lila's grin widened. "Told you. Everything down here tastes like that. Stronger flavor. Better yield. We get lab results back every quarter—higher nutrient density across the board."

Amara swallowed, eyes still scanning the space. "And you don't think that's worth questioning."

"Of course we questioned it," Lila said, shrugging. "Then we stopped worrying and started planning. We used to ration fresh produce in winter. Now we're exporting. We've got reserves that could last years."

She gestured around them, palms open. "This place feeds people. It keeps them steady. Kids grow up eating better than most adults ever did."

Amara wiped her hands on a paper towel and looked at Lila fully. "And what do you think is making this possible."

Lila's expression stayed open, sincere. "I think we found a way to grow here when everyone else gave up on it. I think that matters."

Amara glanced back at the plants, at the heavy fruit, the thick vines, the heat pressing up from below the floor.

"And if the reason matters more than the result?" she asked.

Lila hesitated just long enough for Amara to notice. Then she smiled again, softer this time. "You scientists always want the why. We just needed something that worked."

"Or a symptom."

Lila's smile faded. "A symptom of what?"

"Something changing the environment. Something changing all of us."

"You sound like your mother."

The words hit like a slap.

Amara's voice went cold. "What did you say?"

"Your mother. She used to come down here sometimes. She'd walk through the growing zones and tell me it was wrong. That plants shouldn't grow like this. That we shouldn't trust it." Lila's expression softened. "I liked your mother. But she was scared of progress."

"She was scared of being changed without consent."

"We're all changing. That's what living things do. Adapt or die."

"And what if adaptation isn't evolution? What if it's infection?"

Lila didn't answer immediately. She turned and walked to a wall, pressed her palm against it. The concrete was smooth and warm.

"Feel this," she said.

Amara joined her, placing her own hand on the wall.

Warmth radiated through the material. Not surface heat. *Deep* heat, rising from below.

"It's alive, isn't it?" Lila said quietly. "Whatever's down here. Whatever's generating all this. It's not machinery. It's not geothermal. It's something living."

"You know."

"I've suspected for years. Everyone has. We just don't talk about it." Lila pulled her hand away.

"Because what would we say? That something beneath the town is keeping us alive? That we're dependent on something we don't understand? That stopping it would kill us all?"

"So, you just accept it."

"I accept that my children are healthy. That no one goes hungry. That we've built something sustainable in a world that's collapsing everywhere else." She met Amara's eyes. "Your mother couldn't accept that. It killed her. Don't let it kill you too."

"She died because she refused to change."

"She died because she fought too hard. Sometimes survival means letting go."

Amara stepped back. "Letting go of what? Humanity?"

"Letting go of what you think humanity is supposed to be. Maybe this is who we're becoming. Maybe that's okay."

"It's not okay if we don't get to choose."

"We're choosing every day we stay." Lila gestured around the growing zone. "Look at this. Really look. This isn't death. This isn't disease. This is *abundance.* This is life finding a way."

Amara looked.

The plants were beautiful. Healthy. Thriving in conditions that should be impossible.

Beneath the soil and concrete, beneath the careful insulation and curated warmth, something older than the town continued its quiet labor. It didn't rush. It didn't demand permission. It shaped conditions, adjusted tolerances, prepared bodies and systems alike for what came next. The future it offered arrived disguised as abundance.

"I need to go," Amara said.

Lila turned, surprise flickering across her face. "Wait—"

"Thank you for showing me," Amara said, already backing away. "I mean that. But I'm done here."

She headed for the stairs, boots striking metal with sharp intent. Behind her, Lila followed a few steps, voice raised just enough to carry.

"Amara. You can't fight this."

Amara didn't slow. "Watch me."

She climbed through the lower levels, past rows of dense foliage and hanging fruit, past workers moving between beds with relaxed efficiency. A few glanced up and smiled. Someone waved. Their skin shone with heat and health, their movements easy, practiced. This place had taught them how to belong.

Higher up, the air thinned. The plants changed. Leaves narrowed. The scent of damp soil gave way to cold metal and glass. She pushed through the upper greenhouse doors, where winter leaked through seams and joints, thin and sharp.

Outside, snow fell cleanly from the sky.

Amara stepped into it and stood still, letting the cold bite her cheeks, her hands, her lungs. She drew in breath after breath, searching for that familiar sting, the boundary that told her where her body ended and the world began.

Heat lingered anyway.

It rose through her boots. It pressed up from the pavement. It followed her, subtle and persistent, carried through pipes and roots and stone. Beneath the streets, beneath the houses and greenhouses and carefully kept lives, the source continued its steady cycle.

She could feel it now without touching it.

With every moment she stayed, the town adjusted her. Softened resistance. Rewrote thresholds. Made space for her within its balance.

Amara clenched her jaw and started walking, snow crunching underfoot, cold sharp against her skin. She pulled out her phone and didn't bother waiting for the screen to fully brighten before dialing.

"Tunde," she said the moment the call connected. "I need to talk to you. Now. Meet me at my mother's house."

He started to say her name.

She ended the call and slipped the phone back into her pocket.

The walk home cut straight through the heart of town. Snow dropped in clean, vertical lines, steady and uniform, brushing her shoulders and clinging to her hair. Streetlights cast pale columns through it, turning the sidewalks into narrow corridors of light and shadow. The cold settled over her from above, heavy and compressing, the kind that forced breath shorter and sharper.

Beneath her boots, the ground held its quiet warmth.

She felt it with every step—subtle, persistent, rising through concrete and packed earth, a constant presence she could no longer pretend belonged to chance. It waited beneath the streets and houses, beneath the routines and explanations, patient in the way only something long-established could afford to be.

Grayhaven moved around that warmth without question. People adjusted. Bodies adapted. Language softened around it. What once would have raised alarms had been folded into daily life, renamed comfort, renamed success.

She walked faster, jaw tight, snow melting along her collar.

This place wasn't failing. It wasn't slipping into ruin.

It was changing its terms.

Now that she could feel it—now that her body had begun to register what the town expected of it—there was no neutral ground left. She would either resist with everything she had left, or be carried forward by a transformation she never consented to.

The house came into view ahead, its windows glowing too warmly against the snow. Amara didn't slow. Whatever choice waited inside, she was done pretending it hadn't already been placed in her hands.

# At What Cost

Tunde arrived twenty minutes after Amara called him.

She let him in without a word and walked back to the kitchen, where she'd been sitting with her hand submerged in a bowl of ice water.

"What are you doing?" he asked, stopping in the doorway.

"Testing."

"Testing what?"

She pulled her hand out. The skin was red, fingers stiff. She set a timer on her phone. "How long it takes to recover."

"Amara—"

"Sit down. Please."

He sat across from her, concern etched into his face. "What's going on?"

She watched her hand. The redness was already fading. Her fingers, which should have been numb for at least ten minutes, were flexing normally after three.

She showed him the timer. "Three minutes. Yesterday it took seven. The day before, it took twelve."

Tunde's expression shifted—something resigned settling over his features. "So you're adapting."

"I don't want to adapt. I want to stay myself."

"Those might be the same thing."

"They're not." She stood and started pacing. "This morning I walked to the clinic without gloves. Not because I forgot them. Because I *didn't think I needed them.* Do you understand how terrifying that is? My brain is already changing what it considers dangerous."

"That's not your brain. That's your body learning to survive."

"Without asking permission."

"Bodies don't ask permission. They just try not to die." Tunde leaned back in his chair. "What did you want to talk about?"

Amara stopped pacing and faced him. "I went underground. Into the old shaft beneath the municipal building."

His expression hardened. "When?"

"Last night. With Cruz."

"Jesus, Amara."

"I saw it, Tunde. The organism. Whatever it is that's been under this town the whole time." She watched his face carefully. "You knew. Didn't you?"

He was quiet for a long moment. Then: "I suspected."

"That's not an answer."

"It's the only one I have." He stood and walked to the window, looking out at the snow. "Five years ago, we were digging the eastern corridor extension. Hit something at seventy feet that wasn't rock. Wasn't concrete. Something... organic. The engineer wanted to stop. I told him to dig around it."

"Why?"

"Because stopping meant asking questions no one wanted to answer. Because the warmth was helping us survive. Because..." He turned to face her. "Because I was afraid of what would happen if we interfered."

"People have a right to know."

"People have a right to live. And everyone in this town—everyone who's adapted—depends on that thing now. Symbiosis, Cruz called it. We can't survive without it anymore."

Amara's hands clenched. "So, we just accept being changed? Being remade into something else?"

"We accept being alive."

"At what cost?"

"At whatever cost it takes." Tunde's voice rose slightly. "Do you know how many towns like this used to exist? Places on the edge, barely hanging on? They're gone now. Dead or abandoned. But we're still here. Thriving. That matters."

"Not if we're not human anymore."

"Define human."

"People who get to choose their own evolution."

"Then humans have been extinct for millennia. We've never controlled our evolution. Environment does. Pressure does. Survival does." He moved toward her. "This is just faster. That's the only difference."

"Speed is everything. Evolution takes generations because it gives species time to understand what they're becoming. This—" She gestured around, at the house, the town, everything. "This is theft."

"Or gift." Tunde's voice softened. "Amara, I know this is hard. I know it feels wrong. But look at what we've built. Look at the children who'll grow up never knowing what it means to freeze. To starve. To abandon their homes because the world became unlivable."

"They'll grow up never knowing what it means to be human."

"Maybe that's okay."

The words hung between them.

Amara sat down heavily. "My mother fought this."

"I know."

"It killed her."

"I know that too."

"And you didn't warn me."

Tunde's expression cracked slightly. "I thought you'd leave before it mattered. I thought you'd attend the funeral, sell the house, and go back to your life. I didn't think you'd stay long enough to..." He trailed off.

"To start changing."

"Yeah."

Amara looked at her hands. They looked normal. Felt normal. But underneath, at the cellular level, they were being remade into something that could survive conditions no human should tolerate.

"Can it be reversed?" she asked quietly.

"I don't know. Cruz might know."

"If I leave now—if I cross the snowline and stay out there—will my body revert?"

Tunde was quiet.

"Tunde."

"I don't know," he said finally. "But I know people who've tried. People who left and came back a few months later."

"And?"

"They came back because being out there hurt more than being here. Their bodies couldn't regulate temperature the way they used to. Couldn't handle normal warmth. They'd adapted too far to fit anywhere else."

Amara's stomach dropped. "So it's irreversible."

"Past a certain point, yeah. Maybe."

"How long do I have?"

"I don't know. Everyone's different. Your mother lasted years before her body rejected it. Some people adapt completely in months."

"What about me?"

"You've been here a week. You're already showing changes. If I had to guess..." He hesitated. "Maybe another week before it locks in. Maybe less."

One week.

Seven days to decide between staying and becoming something else, or leaving and risking the same fate that killed her mother—rejection, misalignment, a body caught between two states with nowhere to belong.

"I need air," Amara said, standing abruptly.

"It's fifteen below out there."

"I know."

She grabbed her coat—thinner than the one she'd arrived in, she realized with a spike of fear—and walked outside.

Cold brushed her face as she stepped into the street, sharp enough to wake her skin but gentle where it used to be cruel. Air slid into her lungs cleanly. Her breath came out in pale clouds that drifted and vanished without effort. The sting carried clarity instead of punishment.

Her boots broke the packed snow with a steady crunch, the sound echoing down the empty block. Houses stood tucked into themselves, roofs bowed under white weight, windows glowing with contained warmth. The streetlights cast narrow columns through the falling snow, each one a quiet marker she passed without slowing.

A week ago, this walk would have demanded grit. Every step would have scraped at her chest, tightened her throat, reminded her body of its limits.

Now her muscles moved easily. Her stride held rhythm without strain. The cold registered and released.

She stopped in the center of the road and tugged off her gloves. Snow drifted past her wrists as she lifted her hands into the open air. Skin prickled. Blood rushed forward, flushing her fingers a healthy pink. Sensation stayed intact—pressure, temperature, control.

She counted by breath. Thirty seconds. A minute. Two.

No ache bloomed. No loss crept in.

She pulled the gloves back on and kept walking.

At the edge of town, the street widened and thinned into open road. Beyond it, the world shifted. Snow fell differently there—less disciplined, less certain. The boundary waited ahead, invisible but exact, marking the return of ordinary weather and uninterrupted signal and people who had never learned to live inside this altered balance.

Her car sat parked behind her. Escape rested within reach.

She pictured the drive: tires humming over cleared pavement, the snow thinning mile by mile, the sudden return of radio static resolving into voices. She imagined calling someone—anyone—and hearing disbelief crack into urgency. She imagined telling the story and watching faces change.

Her body answered the thought with a subtle warmth, steady and calm, as if resisting the image.

And after that? Years spent monitoring herself. Testing thresholds. Measuring distance from heat. Living the way her mother had—alert, isolated, quietly out of sync. A body that refused ease. A life shaped by resistance rather than belonging.

She looked back toward town.

Warmth gathered there, distributed through homes and streets and systems that had learned how to accommodate it. People laughed inside that warmth. Children grew into it. Lives rooted themselves deep, sheltered from a future the rest of the world still feared.

She faced forward again, then back once more, caught between paths that both demanded surrender.

Amara turned around and headed toward her mother's house.

The decision didn't settle. It stayed loose, unresolved, carried forward with her steps.

Snow brushed her face again. Cold touched her skin and passed without consequence. With each breath, her body adjusted a little faster, a little more willingly. Somewhere beneath the ground, something continued its quiet work, indifferent to hesitation.

The space to decide narrowed, and it did so without asking.

Amara opened the door before Tunde could knock again.

Cold clung to him, caught in the wool of his coat and the edges of his hair. Snow slid from his shoulders onto the mat, already dissolving as the house pulled heat toward itself. He stepped inside and froze, like he expected the walls to react.

"You went out there," he said. His voice sounded thinner than she'd heard it before.

"Yes."

His eyes tracked her face, searching for something steady to latch onto. "You saw it."

"Yes."

He shut the door too hard. The latch rattled. He exhaled sharply and dragged a hand down his face, leaving moisture behind. "You shouldn't have gone that far."

Amara crossed her arms. "You knew where it ended. You just didn't think I'd follow the line."

"That's different," he snapped, then stopped himself. He turned away, pacing two steps into the living room before stopping short. The heat pressed in on both of them, thick and immediate. "People don't go looking for proof here. They live."

"They adjust," Amara said. "They stop asking questions."

Tunde laughed once, sharp and humorless. "Because asking doesn't change anything."

"It changed my mother."

The words landed harder than she intended. She didn't soften them.

Tunde flinched. His shoulders tightened, then sagged. "You think I don't know that?" he said, voice rising despite his effort to contain it. "You think I don't replay it every winter?"

He rubbed his hands together, skin reddening as the house continued to warm. "She scared people. Meetings. Letters. Charts no one wanted to read. She talked about thresholds and tolerance like we were already halfway gone."

"And she was right," Amara said.

He shook his head, fast. "She was early."

"She was ignored."

He turned on her then, eyes bright, breath uneven. "Do you know what happens if this stops? If someone decides to shut it down or dig it up or move it?" His hands trembled as he gestured toward the floor. "The heat disappears. The crops fail. The boundary collapses. People freeze in their houses because their bodies already adapted."

Amara stepped closer. "So you chose comfort over consent."

"I chose survival," he shot back. "I chose kids who don't cough blood every winter. I chose homes that stay standing."

"You chose to let something else decide for them."

Tunde's voice broke. "What was I supposed to do?"

The house creaked softly, responding to the tension with another subtle adjustment. Warm air rolled through the vents, insistent, enclosing.

Amara picked up the notebook from the table and pressed it into his hands. "She documented everything. She tracked the changes in herself because no one else would. She died believing she failed."

Tunde stared at the cover. His grip tightened, knuckles paling. "She didn't fail," he said, almost pleading. "We failed her."

"Then stop pretending this is neutral," Amara said. "Stop acting like adaptation is harmless."

He swallowed, eyes shining now. "I wake up some mornings and can't tell if the cold feels different or if I do," he said. "Do you know how terrifying that is? To realize your body already made the choice before you did?"

Amara didn't answer. She watched his hands shake, watched the heat bead along his hairline.

Then the house reacted.

A sharp click came from the wall, followed by a rush through the vents that arrived faster than before, fuller. Warm air surged into the room in a single, heavy push. The lights dimmed for a fraction of a second and steadied again.

Tunde flinched. "Did you touch the thermostat?"

"No."

Another sound followed—water, somewhere behind the walls. A brief rush, then a steady drip that landed too quickly to be condensation. The smell shifted with it. Damp plaster. Heated metal.

Amara moved first, crossing the room toward the hallway. "Basement."

They took the stairs two at a time. Heat thickened with each step down. The concrete floor at the bottom glistened, a thin stream of water tracing its way from the utility closet toward the drain. A pipe along the wall sweated visibly, moisture beading and running in uneven lines.

Tunde crouched and pressed his fingers to the metal. He jerked his hand back. "That's hotter than it should be."

Amara followed the line of the pipe with her eyes. It fed into the house like a vein, branching upward, distributing warmth without pause. The drip quickened, water striking concrete with soft, insistent taps.

"This is new," she said.

Tunde stared at the pipe, chest rising fast. "It's accelerating."

The word settled between them, heavier than the argument upstairs.

The overhead light flickered again. Somewhere above, a floorboard popped under pressure. The house adjusted, correcting for a load it hadn't been designed to carry.

Amara straightened slowly. "It's responding."

"To what," Tunde asked, though his voice suggested he already knew.

"To awareness," she said. "To disruption."

They stood there in the damp heat, listening to water gather and move, watching the system strain to accommodate a change that hadn't been requested.

# The Newcomer

The community center sat in the town square—a low, brick building with narrow windows and a metal roof bowed under snow. Amara had passed it dozens of times without going inside.

Today, she needed to see someone else struggling. Someone who wasn't already adapted. Someone who still felt the cold the way she used to.

The interior was warmer than expected, heated by a large wood stove in the center of the main room. A dozen people sat in clusters—some reading, some talking quietly, a few children playing with blocks in the corner.

At a table near the window, a woman sat alone, a mug of something steaming in front of her, a book open but unread.

Amara recognized her from Cruz's charts. Mina Park. Arrived three months ago from Seattle. Still adjusting.

"Mind if I sit?" Amara asked.

The woman looked up—Korean, maybe early thirties, dark hair pulled into a ponytail, eyes tired but sharp. "Go ahead."

Amara sat and gestured at the mug. "What is it?"

"Tea. Or what passes for tea here. Some kind of root thing Lila grows underground." Mina took a sip and grimaced. "It's awful, but it's warm."

"How long have you been here?"

"Three months. You?"

"A week."

Mina's eyes widened slightly. "And you're already asking questions."

"How did you know I was going to ask questions?"

"Because you have that look. Like you're trying to figure out if everyone else is crazy or if you are." She set down her mug. "I had that look for the first month."

"And now?"

"Now I'm just tired."

Amara glanced at the window. Outside, snow fell in those same methodical lines. "Why did you come here?"

"Work. I'm a teacher. They needed one. The pay was good and I wanted to get away from the city." She laughed bitterly. "Turns out I traded one kind of cold for another."

"Do you regret it?"

"I don't know yet. Ask me in another month." Mina studied her. "You're Okoye's daughter, aren't you?"

"Yeah."

"I met her once. She came to the school to drop off books. We talked for maybe five minutes, but..." Mina trailed off. "She seemed sad."

"She was."

"I'm sorry."

"Thank you."

They sat in comfortable silence for a moment. Then Amara said, "Can I ask you something?"

"Sure."

"How do you feel? Physically?"

Mina frowned. "What do you mean?"

"The cold. How does it affect you?"

"Oh." She considered. "It's strange. When I first got here, it was unbearable. I couldn't stay outside for more than a few minutes. I thought I'd made a terrible mistake." She wrapped her hands around her mug. "But it's getting easier. I can walk to school now without feeling like I'm dying. I don't layer as much. My hands don't go numb as fast."

"Does that scare you?"

"Should it?"

"I don't know. Does it?"

Mina was quiet for a moment. "Sometimes I notice things and think 'that's weird.' Like yesterday, I realized I'd been standing outside talking to another teacher for ten minutes and I hadn't been cold at all. I was wearing a fleece. Just a fleece. In February." She looked at Amara. "But then I think, well, that's good, right? I'm adapting. That's what humans do."

"What if it's not adaptation? What if it's something else?"

"Like what?"

"I don't know. Change. Forced change."

Mina's expression grew guarded. "What are you asking?"

"I'm asking if you've noticed that everyone here is different. That children play outside in conditions that should kill them. That the ground is warm when it should be frozen. That something about this town doesn't make sense."

"Of course it doesn't make sense. But nothing makes sense anymore. Seattle was on fire last summer. Phoenix is abandoned. Half the country is either flooding or drought-stricken." Mina's voice rose slightly. "If this town has figured out how to survive, why question it?"

"Because survival without consent isn't survival. It's conversion."

"Consent." Mina laughed sharply. "The planet didn't ask for my consent when it started collapsing. Climate didn't ask permission before it made my hometown unlivable. Why should I demand consent from whatever's keeping me alive here?"

"Because you're human. Because you should get to choose."

"I did choose. I chose to come here. I chose to stay." Mina stood abruptly. "And I choose not to look too closely at how the magic trick works, because knowing won't change anything except how well I sleep at night."

She walked away, leaving her mug and book behind.

Amara sat with her hands wrapped around a paper cup, the tea inside still breathing out thin ribbons of steam. She had forgotten about it somewhere between sitting down and letting the room settle around her. The chair creaked faintly beneath her weight. The community center smelled like citrus cleaner and damp wool, warmth layered thick enough to blur the edges of winter outside.

Laughter cut through the quiet. High, loose, uncontained.

She looked up. A small knot of children had claimed the corner by the foam mats, coats piled in a careless heap. One girl—maybe six—spun in a tight circle, hair sticking to her cheeks, sleeves pushed up past her elbows. At some point she had shed her sweater entirely. She played in a thin T-shirt, skin flushed with heat and movement, utterly at ease.

A woman nearby noticed and crossed the room, hand brushing the girl's shoulder. "Hey, sweetheart. Put your sweater back on."

The girl barely paused. "I'm fine, Mama."

"I know." The woman held out the sweater anyway. "Still."

The child dragged it on with exaggerated effort, lips pushed forward in protest, then bolted back to the game without missing a beat.

The woman caught Amara's gaze and gave a smile that carried fatigue more than apology. "They run warm," she said. "All of them do now."

Amara tilted her head. "That sits okay with you?"

The smile thinned. The woman glanced back at the children, then down at her own hands. "Everything sits heavy if you let it," she said. "She eats. She sleeps. She laughs like that." A small shrug. "I hold onto what I can."

Choice, Amara thought. The word stayed lodged behind her teeth.

She rose and drifted toward the window. Outside, snow slid down in straight, patient lines, collecting on benches and railings that no one bothered to clear until morning. The glass reflected her faintly—lighter coat than she'd worn days ago, hands uncovered, posture easy. Her face carried a calm she hadn't earned.

She looked settled.

The realization tightened her chest.

Behind her, the children shrieked and tumbled. The woman resumed her watch, eyes alert, hands ready, questions folded away beneath routine. The building absorbed their heat without comment, adjusted itself around their presence, encouraged it.

Amara pressed her palm to the window. Cold seeped into her skin, sharp but shallow, passing through without resistance. She pulled her hand back and stared at it, fingers steady.

She left the cup where it sat and walked out.

Snow met her immediately. Cold gathered around her face and shoulders, weight pressing from above. She crossed the street and kept going, boots finding their rhythm, breath even.

The weather carried the shape of hardship without the cost.

Thoughts followed her anyway. They clung, persistent, settling along the edges of her mind.

One week.

Maybe less.

Time moved forward, indifferent to her hesitation. Somewhere beneath the streets, something continued to prepare the ground for what came next.

Amara walked on, unsure what she would choose when the moment finally closed.

Her boot caught on something solid and unyielding.

She windmilled, arms flailing, dignity abandoning her immediately, and managed to catch herself against a streetlight with a graceless grunt. Snow puffed up around her ankles in a soft explosion.

She froze, heart pounding, then glanced around.

No witnesses. Of course.

She straightened slowly, brushing at her coat like that had all been intentional. "Smooth," she muttered to herself, then snorted. The sound surprised her enough that she laughed—an actual laugh, loud and short and a little unhinged.

She looked down at the culprit.

A snowbank. Shaped into something suspiciously geometric. Someone had carved steps into it. Tiny ones. Uneven. The work of children with too much confidence and not enough planning.

Amara stared at it, then shook her head. "OSHA would shut you down so fast," she said to the snow.

The snow, predictably, offered no defense.

She stepped around it carefully this time, still smiling, breath fogging the air as the laughter lingered longer than she expected. The sound felt good. Necessary. Like proof she hadn't turned into a walking crisis response.

A porch light flicked on nearby. Someone opened a door and called out, "Hey! You okay?"

Amara lifted a hand in a quick wave. "Yep. Lost a fight with public infrastructure."

The door closed. The light stayed on.

She walked the rest of the block grinning to herself, shaking her head, letting the ridiculousness of it settle her nerves. The town had secrets buried deep beneath it. Ancient forces. Impossible choices.

And also children building snow stairs with reckless optimism.

"Get it together," she told herself gently, still smiling.

The smile stayed as she walked, loosening only when the street shifted under her feet. Snow here had been packed smooth by traffic and boots, then reheated just enough to soften the top layer. Her steps left shallow impressions that filled in behind her, edges rounding as if the ground disliked sharp marks.

A pair of teenagers skidded past on a plastic sled, shrieking as they overshot the corner and slammed into a snowbank. One of them popped up immediately, laughing, cheeks flushed, hat hanging crooked around his neck.

"Again!" he yelled.

The other groaned. "My tailbone votes no."

They dragged the sled back uphill anyway.

Amara stepped aside to let them pass, catching the smell of wet plastic and sweat and winter coats that had been worn too long indoors. One of the kids nodded at her, breathless, like she was part of the landscape rather than a stranger passing through it.

She nodded back.

Farther down the block, a storefront window glowed green and yellow, the little grocery still open late. A handwritten sign taped to the glass announced fresh oranges, three for a dollar. Oranges. In a town buried under constant snow. She paused just long enough to register it, then kept moving.

Steam curled from a storm drain ahead, rising straight before dissolving. The metal grate around it sat warm enough to melt a clean ring into the snow. Someone had set a paper cup there, empty now, balanced right at the edge of the cleared circle like an offering.

Her mother would have noticed that.

Amara slowed, then forced herself to keep walking.

The houses grew closer together near her street, porches nearly touching, lights glowing behind curtains. She passed a row of boots lined up outside a door, all damp, all steaming faintly as heat escaped from inside. Laughter drifted out when the door opened briefly, followed by a rush of warm air that chased her down the sidewalk before retreating.

She reached her mother's house and stopped, hand hovering over the gate latch. Snow had gathered on the railing again, smooth and undisturbed since she'd left. The porch boards radiated a quiet, steady warmth through her soles.

Amara exhaled and stepped inside the yard.

Behind her, the town kept moving—sleds scraping, doors opening and closing, heat rising and spreading without effort.

The sound folded into another memory before she could stop it.

She was younger then, still short enough that her mother's stride forced her into a half-run. Snow had come early that year too, clinging stubbornly to the sidewalks, refusing to melt even when the sun tried. Amara remembered complaining about it, about the way the cold bit her ears and turned her nose pink.

Her mother had laughed and tightened her scarf.

"Cold is not an enemy," she said, the words braided together with the rhythm of home. "Ọ na-akụ, yes, but it teaches you where your body ends."

They walked like that often—slow circuits around the neighborhood, her mother's gloved hand firm around Amara's wrist. It was how she checked the town without making it obvious. How she listened without standing still.

That afternoon, they stopped by the old footbridge near the creek, the one everyone pretended was decorative even though it served no real purpose. Steam drifted up from the water below, thin and quiet.

Amara had leaned over the railing and frowned. "Why is it warm?"

Her mother didn't answer right away. She rested her elbows on the railing beside her daughter and stared down at the water, eyes sharp, calculating.

"Mm," she murmured. "You noticed that."

"Of course I noticed," Amara said. "It smells different too."

Her mother smiled then, a brief, private thing. "Ị bụ nwa m," she said. "You pay attention."

She reached into her coat pocket and pulled out a small notebook, edges softened from use. She flipped it open and jotted something down—date, time, location. Always the same neat columns. Always the same patience.

"What are you writing?" Amara asked.

"Questions," her mother said. "And answers that don't admit they are answers yet."

Amara wrinkled her nose. "That doesn't make sense."

Her mother laughed again. "Most important things don't, at first."

They started walking again, their steps crunching in sync. Snow fell in straight lines then too, though Amara hadn't known to think of it that way yet. She only knew it felt heavy, pressing down from the sky as if the clouds themselves were tired.

"Ma," she said after a while. "Why don't you wear your hat?"

Her mother touched her hair, thick and coiled, uncovered despite the cold. "Because I need to feel when it changes."

"Changes how?"

"Subtly," she replied. "Like a warning whispered too softly."

Amara frowned. "You always say things like that."

Her mother stopped walking and crouched to her level, snow soaking into the knees of her pants. She took Amara's face gently between her hands, thumbs warm against her cheeks.

"Listen to me," she said, voice shifting fully into Igbo without thinking. "Ụwa adịghị asọpụrụ mmadụ. The world does not ask permission. It pushes. It adapts you. If you do not feel it, you will wake up already changed."

Amara swallowed. "That's scary."

"Yes," her mother said simply. "So we learn early."

They reached home just as the streetlights flicked on, orange halos glowing through falling snow. Her mother paused at the gate, eyes scanning the block. Heat spilled from the houses around them, doors opening briefly, laughter carrying on the air.

"Why does everyone else look… fine?" Amara asked.

Her mother rested a hand on the fence. "Because fine is a wide word," she said. "It holds many truths people don't examine."

Inside, the house had been too warm even then. Her mother moved through it with practiced efficiency—turning vents down, cracking a window despite the cold. Amara remembered shivering and complaining.

"You'll thank me later," her mother had said, handing her a mug of tea. Ginger and honey. Sharp enough to clear her sinuses.

They sat at the kitchen table while the kettle cooled. Her mother spread papers out—weather logs, utility bills, hand-drawn maps of the town with certain areas circled in red.

"Do you ever wish we lived somewhere else?" Amara asked suddenly.

Her mother looked up, surprised. "Why?"

"Because everyone here feels… different."

Her mother studied her for a long moment. Then she reached across the table and squeezed Amara's hand.

"We go where our work is," she said. "And sometimes, our work is to leave records behind."

"Records for who?"

"For whoever comes next and refuses to accept easy answers."

Amara had sighed dramatically, resting her chin in her hands. "You make everything sound like homework."

Her mother smiled, tired but fond. "It is," she said. "For the soul."

Later that night, Amara woke to the sound of movement downstairs. She crept to the top of the stairs and watched her mother pacing the living room, notebook open, pen moving quickly. The thermostat glowed behind her, numbers lowered again.

Her mother paused, sensing her presence without turning. "Go back to bed, nwa m."

"Are you worried?" Amara asked.

Her mother hesitated. "I am alert."

"That sounds like worried."

A soft laugh. "Perhaps."

She knelt in front of Amara and brushed her hair back. "If the ground ever feels warmer than it should," she said quietly, "promise me you won't ignore it."

Amara nodded, solemn. "I promise."

"Good." Her mother kissed her forehead. "Now sleep. Tomorrow we measure again."

The memory loosened its grip slowly, like fingers unclenching.

Amara stood in the yard now, snow settling on her shoulders, warmth rising through the soles of her boots. Her mother's voice lingered with clarity she hadn't expected.

If you do not feel it, you will wake up already changed.

Amara looked down at her hands. Bare earlier than they should have been. Steady. Adapted.

"I feel it," she whispered, unsure who she was answering anymore.

The house waited behind her. The town breathed around her. And somewhere beneath it all, the ground held its heat, unchanged by memory, indifferent to promises.

Her mother had been right. The world did not ask permission.

Amara was running out of time to decide how she would answer back.

# The Child

Isaac Reed found her without announcing himself. One moment the bench creaked under her weight alone, the next there was a presence beside her, close enough to register warmth.

"Hi," he said.

Amara jumped despite herself. "Isaac—hey."

He smiled, pleased but unbothered. "Sorry. I didn't mean to scare you."

"It's fine." She shifted, making space. "What are you doing back here?"

He pointed vaguely toward the yard. "Walking around."

"In this?" She gestured at the snow drifting down around them.

He shrugged and climbed onto the bench, sneakers brushing the wood, legs swinging freely. "I like how quiet it gets."

She glanced at him properly then. Hoodie. Jeans. Sneakers soaked through at the seams. No coat. No gloves. His cheeks held a steady pink, the color of exertion rather than exposure.

"Aren't you cold?" she asked.

He paused, thinking it over. "Maybe? I don't really feel it the way other people talk about it."

Amara watched his breath fog faintly, then clear. "You know it's fifteen below."

His eyebrows lifted. "Is it?"

"Yes."

"Oh." He tipped his head back to watch the snow fall. "Mr. Bello says numbers matter. I always forget to ask what they mean."

Her fingers curled against the bench. "How old are you, Isaac?"

"Eight." He grinned. "Almost nine. My birthday's in March. Or April. I keep mixing it up."

"And you've lived here the whole time."

"Yeah. Born here." He nodded toward the clinic visible through the trees. "Dr. Cruz pulled me out. Dad says I came fast."

She swallowed. "Have you ever gone anywhere else?"

He shook his head without hesitation. "We tried once."

Her attention sharpened. "Tried where."

"To Vermont. My grandma lives there." His legs swung a little faster now. "Dad drove for a long time. We got close. Past the farms."

"And?"

Isaac scrunched his nose. "I felt bad."

"In what way."

"Like my head was spinning." He pressed a hand flat to his chest. "And hot. Too hot. Like when you stand too close to the vent."

Amara's voice came out carefully. "What did your dad do."

"He turned around." Isaac said it like a punchline. "He said the air wasn't right for me. Said my body didn't like it."

"Did you see your grandma."

"Nope." He didn't sound disappointed. Just factual. "She sends cards."

Amara stared out at the yard, at the snow gathering along the fence line, the bench legs sinking deeper into softened ground. "How long did it take to feel better."

"Right away," Isaac said. "As soon as we crossed back."

"Back where."

He smiled at her, open and sincere. "Here."

Silence stretched between them, filled by the soft hiss of falling snow.

"Do you ever want to go somewhere else?" she asked.

He considered this more seriously. His feet slowed. "Sometimes I think about oceans. They look cold too."

"And then."

"Then I think about how warm it must get there." He made a face. "And I stop."

He turned to her, studying her expression with quiet focus. "You've been places, right."

"Yes."

"Places where the snow doesn't stay."

"Yes."

"Did you like it."

She hesitated. The bench creaked beneath her as she shifted. "I did."

His eyes narrowed slightly, curious rather than judgmental. "Why'd you come back."

The question landed clean and heavy.

Amara exhaled slowly. "Because my mother lived here."

"Oh." He nodded, accepting that as sufficient. "She sat here a lot."

Her breath caught. "You remember that."

"Yeah." Isaac smiled faintly. "She talked to the ground. Not like people talk to people. Different."

Amara stared straight ahead. "What did she say."

He shrugged. "I don't know. Grown-up stuff."

Snow brushed against his hair and melted immediately. He didn't react.

"Amara," he said after a moment.

"Yes."

"Do you think people can be made for places."

Her chest tightened. "I think places try very hard to make people fit them."

He seemed satisfied with that. He hopped down from the bench, landing lightly.

"I should go," he said. "Dad worries when I stay out too long."

She nodded. "Thanks for sitting with me."

"Anytime." He took a few steps, then turned back. "You feel different than when you got here."

Her throat went dry. "Different how."

He tilted his head, thinking. "Like you're warmer inside now."

Then he waved and trotted off toward the house, sneakers leaving shallow prints that filled in almost immediately.

Amara stayed where she was, the bench cold beneath her palms, the ground warm beneath her feet, the space between those truths growing harder to ignore.

Isaac nodded like she'd explained something he already knew. "My mom says some people fit here and some people don't," he said. "She says your mom didn't fit."

The words landed with quiet precision.

Amara swallowed. "No," she said. "She didn't."

"I'm sorry." He said it plainly, without softening or distance. "It must be hard to be somewhere that keeps telling you you're wrong."

She let out a slow breath. "Yeah. It is."

They sat together, shoulders nearly touching, snow collecting along the bench slats and the ground beneath their feet. Isaac swung his legs again, heels knocking gently against the wood. He seemed content just being there, eyes tracking the steady fall of white.

"Isaac," Amara said after a moment, keeping her voice level. "Can I ask you something?"

He glanced at her. "Okay."

"Do you know what's under the town?"

His legs stopped mid-swing.

"What do you mean?" he asked, though his posture had already shifted.

"Below the streets," she said. "Below the buildings. What makes it warm down there."

Something closed off behind his eyes. Not fear. Familiarity.

"We're not supposed to talk about that."

"Who told you that?"

He shrugged, shoulders lifting toward his ears. "Everyone. It's just... known."

"Known how?"

He picked at a loose thread on his sleeve. "Like how you don't ask people about scars. Or bodies. It's private."

Amara turned slightly to face him. "You're saying what's under the town is private."

"Kind of," he said. "Mr. Bello says it's what makes Grayhaven special. And special things need protection."

"Protection from what?"

"From being messed up," he said, matter-of-fact. "From people who don't understand them."

She let that sit for a moment. Snow brushed against Isaac's hair and melted without leaving a trace.

"Has anyone taken you down there?" she asked. "Really down there."

He nodded. "Once."

Her pulse picked up. "When."

"School trip. Second grade." He brightened slightly. "We had worksheets."

"What did they tell you it was?"

"Geothermal energy." He recited it cleanly. "The earth holds heat and sometimes it comes closer to the surface."

"And you believed that?"

He made a face. "Not really."

"Why not?"

"Because I looked it up," he said. "And there aren't volcanoes here."

Amara felt a tight, aching pressure behind her eyes. "What did your teacher say when you told her that."

"That science is big," Isaac said. "And sometimes you don't get all the answers."

He looked at her then, earnest and searching. "Do you think that's true?"

She answered without hesitation. "No."

His eyebrows lifted.

"I think answers exist whether people like them or not," she continued. "And saying 'that's just how it is' usually means someone doesn't want to explain."

Isaac considered this carefully. "Then why won't they explain this?"

Amara didn't respond right away. She watched the snow pile at the base of the fence, watched the way the ground beneath it stayed dark and soft.

"Because once you explain something," she said slowly, "you have to decide what to do about it."

"And they already decided," Isaac said.

"Yes."

He leaned back, palms flat on the bench. "My mom says this place keeps us safe."

"Safe from what."

He shrugged again. "From freezing. From being hungry. From going away."

The last one sat heavier.

"Isaac," Amara said gently, "if you wanted to leave—really leave—do you think you could?"

He didn't answer right away. When he did, his voice stayed calm. "I think I'd get sick."

Her chest tightened.

"But I don't want to," he added quickly. "Everyone I know is here."

She nodded. "I know."

He glanced at her sideways. "Do you want to leave?"

Amara looked down at her hands. Bare more often now. Steady. Adapted.

"I don't know," she said honestly.

Isaac seemed satisfied with that. He slid off the bench again, landing lightly, brushing snow from his jeans. "I should go," he said. "Dinner soon."

"Okay."

He took a few steps, then paused. "Amara?"

"Yes."

"You ask questions like my teacher before she stopped."

Her chest tightened, then released in a slow, unfamiliar way, as if something had finally adjusted its grip.

He waved and ran toward the house, boots leaving prints that softened almost immediately.

Amara stayed on the bench, snow settling around her, warmth rising from below, the child's words echoing louder than anything else she'd heard all day.

Some people fit here. Some people don't. The town had already made its preference clear.

"I think something very old lives under this place," Amara said, voice low, almost careful with the words. "Something that's been adjusting us. Getting us ready for something we don't even know is coming yet."

Isaac's eyes went wide, the way they did when a story tipped from boring into interesting. "Like a superhero thing?"

She let out a short breath that almost turned into a laugh. "Something like that."

"Do we get powers?"

"Not the fun kind," she said. "And nobody gets to opt in."

He considered that, rocking back on his heels. "In the good stories, they don't pick," he said finally. "They just figure out what to do after."

She looked at him then, really looked at him. Eight years old. Comfortable in snow that should have punished him. Built perfectly for this place.

"That's one way to think about it," she said.

He hopped down from the bench again, landing lightly. "I gotta go. Mom checks the clock a lot."

"Isaac—wait."

He stopped and turned back, patient.

"Are you happy?" she asked. "Here. Being... this." She gestured vaguely, the word refusing to form. "Are you happy?"

He didn't answer right away. His face scrunched as he searched for something precise. "I think so," he said at last. "I like my friends. I like school. I like how the snow makes everything quiet. I don't know what happy is supposed to feel like, but if this isn't it, I don't know what is."

"And leaving?" she asked. "Does it bother you that you can't?"

He shook his head, genuinely puzzled. "Why would it? This is my home."

Then he waved and ran off, boots kicking up small sprays of powder, footprints forming and softening almost immediately.

Amara stayed on the bench.

The yard felt smaller without him, the quiet heavier. Snow gathered on the slats beside her, on her coat, on her hair. The ground beneath her feet stayed soft and yielding.

Isaac was happy. The children at the community center were happy. Mina Park kept moving forward whether she named it or not. Tunde had learned how to live with the truth by folding himself around it. Cruz stayed and measured and documented, choosing observation over escape.

Everyone had found a way to remain.

Everyone except her mother.

Amara lowered her gaze to her hands resting in her lap. Pink. Steady. Capable. No ache creeping in. No stiffness. They looked like hands that belonged here.

Built for here.

The thought settled uneasily.

She pictured the road beyond the edge of town. The snow thinning. The air shifting. She imagined the heat there pressing in too fast, her pulse racing, her balance slipping. She imagined turning back because her body insisted.

Time tightened around the idea.

A week. Maybe less.

Snow thickened, falling faster now, collecting along her shoulders. She waited for the cold to demand something from her. It never did.

No shiver. No bite. No warning.

Just comfort.

That was the part that frightened her.

Amara stood and went inside, brushing snow from her coat with hands that stayed steady, fingers that didn't ache. The door closed behind her, sealing in warmth that wrapped easily around her frame.

The house held it. The town held it. Below, the steady pulse continued its work.

With every breath she took, the space to choose narrowed again, indifferent to what she wanted, attentive only to what she was becoming.

# Warm Core

Amara went back down alone.

She waited until midnight, when the municipal building would be empty, when no one would see her descend into the sealed shaft that everyone pretended didn't exist.

She needed to see it again. To understand it. To know what was remaking her from the inside out.

The panel came off easier this time—she'd loosened the bolts days ago with Cruz. She swung herself into the shaft and started climbing down, her phone's flashlight clenched between her teeth.

The warmth enveloped her immediately.

A week ago, it had been oppressive. Now it felt almost welcoming. Comfortable.

That shift terrified her.

She descended past the first landing, past the point where concrete gave way to organic walls, into corridors that curved and pulsed with faint bioluminescence. The organism had made this. Grown it. Shaped it deliberately to draw humans deeper.

The chamber opened before her like a cathedral.

The organism filled the space—massive, ancient, alive. Its surface rippled with slow, rhythmic contractions, pulling heat inward and radiating it outward in waves that made the air shimmer.

Amara approached until she stood three feet away.

This close, she could see details she'd missed before. Structures embedded in the larger mass—node-like formations that pulsed with light, thread-thin connections that disappeared into the rock, patterns that repeated at different scales like fractals.

It was beautiful in the way a hurricane was beautiful. Terrible and vast and utterly indifferent to human concern.

She reached out, fingers trembling, and touched it.

The surface was warm. Yielding. Not quite solid, not quite liquid. Her hand sank slightly, and she felt—

*—pulse—*

*—breath—*

*—waiting—*

Not thoughts. Not language. Just sensations. Imperatives. Ancient biological programming executing across incomprehensible timeframes.

*Survive.*

*Adapt.*

*Continue.*

Amara pulled her hand back, gasping.

She'd felt it. Really felt it. Not as a monster or invader, but as something doing what it was designed to do. Ensuring continuity. Bridging gaps. Preparing life for conditions it couldn't survive unaided.

It wasn't evil.

It wasn't even aware of her in any meaningful way.

It was just *doing its job.*

And that made it more terrifying than any malevolence could be.

"You can't stop, can you?" she whispered. "You'll keep changing us until we fit. Until we're ready for whatever's coming."

The organism pulsed, oblivious.

Amara walked around the perimeter of the chamber, studying the way the organism integrated with the rock. There were no clear boundaries—it blended seamlessly, as if it had been here so long it had become part of the geology itself.

How long? Decades? Centuries? Longer?

She found markings on the wall—old, weathered, barely visible. Human markings. Carved into the rock with tools.

She brushed away mineral deposits and read:

*1897. Found this while digging the town well. Warm. Alive. Do not disturb.*

*—J. Mercer*

1897.

The organism had been discovered over a century ago. The town had known. Had built over it. Had benefited from it. Had kept it secret.

For how long had Grayhaven been symbiotic?

Amara kept searching and found more markings.

*1923. Three children born this winter. All healthy. Cold doesn't touch them like it touches me.*

*1945. The town is changing. We are changing. God help us.*

*1968. My son left for college. Came home after six months. Said the world felt wrong. Too hot. Too loud. Too much. He'll never leave again.*

*1982. We've stopped asking why.*

The progression was clear. Each generation more adapted. Each generation more dependent. Each generation less able to imagine life anywhere else.

This wasn't new.

This was the culmination of over a century of slow, patient transformation.

And now it was accelerating.

Amara returned to the organism and stood before it, feeling its heat, watching its slow pulse, understanding finally what her mother had understood years ago.

This thing wasn't changing humanity out of cruelty or malice.

It was doing it because that's what it did.

Like a heart pumping blood. Like lungs pulling oxygen. Like any biological system executing its function without thought or choice.

It prepared species for survival.

It reshaped them for continuity.

And if the reshaping meant they were no longer quite the same species they'd been before—well, survival didn't ask for aesthetic consistency.

"What are you preparing us for?" Amara asked the silent chamber.

The organism moved with its steady rhythm, expansion followed by release, heat rolling outward in slow waves that pressed against the chamber walls. The air thickened with it, heavy enough to feel on her skin, every breath warmed before it reached her lungs.

Something settled deep inside her, low and instinctive, bypassing thought entirely. A vision without images. A pressure without sound. A future shaped by temperature alone.

Cold—far beyond this season, far beyond this latitude. A kind that stripped the surface bare, that punished exposure without pause, that demanded bodies capable of enduring it or disappearing entirely. The chamber seemed to lean into that certainty, its pulse unbroken, unconcerned with timing or permission.

Amara stood very still. She didn't try to name what the thing below understood, or whether understanding was even the right word. She only felt the direction of its work, the patience behind it, the refusal to slow for anything as small as human preference.

Her breath came shallow and warm. Her pulse stayed even.

The truth lodged itself without ceremony: whatever was happening no longer required her agreement.

She turned and started for the passageway.

The climb back felt different this time. Each step carried ease. The heat remained behind her, contained in the chamber, but its imprint stayed close—under her skin, threaded through her blood, carried forward in the way her body regulated itself without effort. Muscles moved smoothly. Breath stayed steady. Balance held.

By the time she reached the basement, the change no longer felt abstract.

She sealed the panel with practiced motions and pushed out into the open air. Snow fell around her in clean lines, brushing her face and settling on her coat. The cold met her and passed through without resistance, registering and releasing as if it belonged there.

She stood for a moment beneath the snowfall, listening to her own breathing.

The lack of pain spoke louder than any warning.

Time, she understood then, had begun to run thin.

She didn't linger outside the building. Snow gathered on her shoulders, melted, gathered again. The pattern repeated without consequence. Amara turned up her collar out of habit rather than need and started walking.

The municipal lot was empty now. Tire tracks softened even as she watched them. Light from the streetlamps bent through falling snow and pooled on the ground, halos steady and calm. The town looked the way it always had—contained, functional, quietly sure of itself.

Her phone vibrated in her pocket.

She stopped walking but didn't pull it out right away. Her pulse stayed even. That alone unsettled her more than the message waiting.

When she finally looked, it was Tunde.

*Did you feel that? The heat spike. The systems adjusted.*

Amara typed back with bare fingers.

*Yes. It's speeding up.*

Three dots appeared. Vanished. Reappeared.

*We'll stabilize it*, Tunde wrote. *We always do.*

Her reply came slower this time. *That's what scares me.*

She slipped the phone away and crossed the street. A group of teenagers clustered near the corner, laughing too loudly, passing around a thermos. Steam lifted from the lid when one of them unscrewed it. They didn't notice the cold. One of them had snow clinging to his hair, melting into his collar without reaction.

"Yo, Amara," someone called. "You want some?"

She shook her head and kept moving. The sound of their laughter clung for a few steps, bounced once off the row of houses, then thinned into the steady hush that blanketed the street. Snow filled the space it left behind, softening edges, lowering the world's volume until only her boots and breath remained.

The block leading to her mother's house felt narrower than it used to. Porches sat close together, railings half-buried, wind chimes frozen in place. Heat bled gently from basements and crawl spaces, lifting faint steam where it met the cold air. It rose from grates, from cracks in the pavement, from places no one bothered to look twice at anymore.

Her shoulders relaxed as she walked. She noticed it only when she tried to pull them back up again.

A neighbor across the street wrestled with a recycling bin, sleeves pushed up, bare forearms flushed and steady. He nodded at her without surprise, as if this weather asked nothing of either of them. She nodded back and kept going.

The house came into view slowly, the familiar shape softened by snow. The porch light flicked on as she reached the gate, casting a warm oval across the steps. It made the falling flakes glow as they passed through it, each one briefly illuminated before disappearing against the boards.

She stopped at the door.

Her hand closed around the knob, and warmth met her palm immediately, traveling through skin and bone with quiet ease. The wood felt alive beneath her touch—held heat, kept it, offered it freely. She stood there longer than necessary, listening to the muted sounds of the town behind her, feeling the house recognize her presence.

Then she drew a breath and turned the knob. Inside, the house greeted her without ceremony. Heat settled along her spine, familiar now. Accepting.

She went straight to the kitchen and poured a glass of water. It tasted clean. Neutral. She drank it all and set the glass down carefully, as if the counter might be watching.

Her mother's notebook sat where she'd left it. Amara picked it up and flipped through pages she knew by heart. Dates. Measurements. Margins crowded with questions that never received replies. Toward the end, the handwriting tightened, lines crowding closer together.

She stopped at a page she hadn't noticed before. No numbers. Just a sentence, written smaller than the rest. *When adaptation becomes comfort, resistance feels like pain.*

Amara closed the notebook.

Upstairs, the house made a soft sound as it adjusted again. Pipes shifted. Vents sighed. The warmth redistributed itself with quiet efficiency.

She moved to the window and looked out at the street. Snow fell heavier now, filling the dark with motion. Somewhere beyond the houses, beyond the boundary, the world still moved under different rules. She could leave. She knew that.

Her body answered the thought with a subtle tightening, not refusal, but hesitation.

"Not yet," she said aloud, surprising herself with the steadiness of it.

Outside, a plow rumbled past, blade scraping, heat rising from the cleared asphalt behind it. The town kept functioning. Kept adapting.

Amara stepped back from the window and reached for her coat. If time was thinning, she wasn't going to spend what remained standing still.

# Adapted to This

Dr. Cruz's office was dark when Amara arrived at 2 a.m., but she knew he'd be there. He'd told her once that he couldn't sleep anymore—that knowing what was under the town had stolen rest from him the way it had stolen certainty.

She knocked anyway.

"Come in," his voice called, muffled.

He sat at his desk, surrounded by papers and open books, a mug of something cold beside him. He looked up as she entered, unsurprised.

"You went back down," he said.

"Yeah."

"Alone?"

"Yeah."

He gestured at the chair across from him. "And?"

Amara sat. "I touched it."

Cruz's eyes widened. "What happened?"

"Nothing. And everything." She struggled to find words. "It's not hostile. It's not even aware of us as individuals. It's just... executing. Like a program. Like biology."

"Did you feel anything?"

"Purpose. Continuity. Instructions older than language." She met his eyes. "It's not from here, is it?"

Cruz shook his head slowly. "I don't think so. I've been researching for years. Trying to find any terrestrial organism with even remotely similar properties. There's nothing. Not in any ecosystem, any geological record, any evolutionary lineage."

"So, it came from somewhere else."

"Or it was put here. Deliberately." He pulled a book toward him—old, leather-bound, pages yellowed. "I found this in the historical society archives. A journal from the town's founding surveyor. He describes finding 'a warm place in the earth, circular and vast, like the heart of something sleeping.'"

"1897," Amara said. "I saw markings down there. Someone named J. Mercer."

"James Mercer. The surveyor." Cruz opened the journal and turned it so she could see. The handwriting was careful, precise. "He recommended they build the town elsewhere. Said the warmth was 'unnatural' and 'potentially dangerous.'"

"But they built anyway."

"Because winter was coming and they were desperate. Because warmth meant survival. Because when you're cold and dying, you don't ask where the fire comes from."

Amara read through the journal entries. Mercer had documented everything—the discovery, his concerns, the council's decision to proceed, the first winter when they'd realized how much easier survival was with the warmth bleeding up from below.

And then, three years later, a final entry:

*The children born here are different. Stronger. Hardier. They play in cold that would kill my generation. I believe the warmth is changing us. I believe this is not accidental. Something beneath the earth is* preparing *us. For what, I do not know. But I fear the cost of this gift will only become clear when it is too late to refuse it.*

"He knew," Amara whispered.

"They all knew, on some level. They just chose survival over certainty." Cruz closed the journal. "Can you blame them?"

"Yes. Because they didn't just choose for themselves. They chose for every generation after."

"That's what survival always does. It binds the future to the present's desperate choices."

Amara stood and walked to the window. Outside, snow fell in perfect lines. The town slept, warm and secure, three feet of snow on every roof and no one worried about collapse.

"What is it?" she asked. "Really. If you had to name it. Define it. What would you call it?"

Cruz was quiet for a long time. Then: "A continuity engine."

"Explain."

"Life on Earth has survived five mass extinction events. Asteroid impacts, super volcanoes, climate collapse, ice ages, anoxic oceans. Every time, something made it through. Not the dominant species—usually they died. But something survived. Something adapted. Something continued."

"You think this organism causes that?"

"No. I think it *enables* it. I think it's part of a system—maybe natural, maybe engineered—that ensures life persists through extinction bottlenecks. It doesn't prevent the catastrophe. It prepares the survivors."

"By changing them."

"By making them compatible with what's coming."

Amara turned to face him. "And what's coming?"

"I don't know. But based on the rate of change, based on how aggressively the organism is accelerating adaptation..." He pulled up a chart on his computer—temperature projections, climate models, feedback loops. "If I had to guess? Collapse. Real collapse. Not just economic or political. Ecological. Atmospheric. A shift in global climate so severe that surface temperatures in the northern hemisphere drop catastrophically."

"Another ice age."

"Or something worse. Something faster. The organism is preparing us for cold that would kill unadjusted humans in minutes. Cold that would make current Arctic conditions look temperate."

"When?"

"Maybe a decade. Maybe a century. The organism doesn't operate on human timeframes. It works in generations."

"And the people here—the children born adapted—they'll survive it."

"Yes."

"While everyone else dies."

Cruz's expression was bleak. "Yes."

Amara sank back into the chair. "We have to warn people."

"Warn them of what? That there's an alien organism under a small town in the north that's preparing locals for a climate catastrophe that might happen eventually? That humanity needs to either move here and adapt, or die when conditions shift?" He laughed bitterly. "They'll call it science fiction. Conspiracy. Mass hysteria."

"Then we show them. We bring evidence. We make them see."

"Amara. The state researcher came here five years ago. She ran tests. Took samples. Found nothing unusual. The organism doesn't show up on instruments the way you'd expect. It's biological, but not in a way our tools can easily measure. It exists in a space between what we call alive and what we call geological."

"Then we bring people down there. Make them touch it like I did."

"And say what? 'Trust me, this ancient alien mass is remaking your biology'? They won't come. And if they do, they'll rationalize it away. Geothermal anomaly. Collective delusion. Anything but the truth."

"So we do nothing?"

"I've been doing nothing for five years. It doesn't feel any better over time."

Amara stood and paced the small office. "There has to be something. Some way to stop it or slow it or at least give people a choice."

"Stop it how? Destroy it? Everyone in Grayhaven dies. Their bodies can't regulate temperature anymore. They're symbiotic." Cruz's voice rose. "And even if you could destroy it, what then? Humanity remains unprepared for what's coming. The organism is awful, yes. But it's also the only reason anyone here will survive."

"Survival isn't everything."

"Tell that to the dead."

They stared at each other in the dim office, the weight of impossible choices pressing down like the snow outside.

Finally, Amara said, "My mother chose to resist."

"And she died."

"But she died *herself.* She died human."

"Human doesn't mean anything if you're dead."

"It means something to the people who remember you."

Cruz looked away. "Maybe."

Amara moved toward the door, then stopped. "If I leave—if I cross the snowline and never come back—will I survive?"

"I don't know. You're already pretty far along. A week, maybe less, and you'll be locked in." He met her eyes. "After that, leaving might kill you. Your body won't tolerate normal temperatures anymore. You'll be like Isaac. Built for here, not there."

“So I’m already trapped.”

Tunde didn’t answer right away. The house filled the pause with small sounds—pipes ticking as heat shifted, the soft rush through the vents correcting itself. When he spoke, his voice came low, scraped thin.

“We all are,” he said. “The only difference is how long you last.”

Amara’s hand closed around the door handle. The metal was warm. Too warm.

“You think it’s that simple,” she said.

“I think pretending otherwise gets people killed.” He ran a hand through his hair, left it there, fingers pressing hard against his scalp. “You leave, your body turns on you. You stay, you adapt. That’s the math.”

She pulled the door open. Cold rushed in, sharp enough to sting her cheeks, snow blowing sideways across the porch.

“There’s another option,” she said.

He frowned. "Which is?"

She stepped into the doorway, half in light, half in snowfall. "Staying and fighting."

His mouth opened, closed again. "Amara—"

She was already outside.

The door shut behind her, cutting off the warmth in a clean line. Snow thickened immediately, falling hard and straight, filling the yard with motion. Cold pressed down from above, heavy and deliberate, settling into her coat, her hair, the space between breaths.

Beneath her boots, the ground held its steady heat.

She felt it through the soles, faint but unmistakable, rising from below the frozen surface. It moved through foundations and pipes and roots, threaded beneath streets and houses and the quiet lives stacked neatly above it. Somewhere deep under the town, the source continued its slow cycle, certain of its work.

It didn't rush her.

It didn't argue.

It only waited.

All it required was time—enough for bodies to adjust, enough for thresholds to shift, enough for resistance to start feeling unnecessary. Enough for choice to erode into habit.

Amara stood in the yard, snow collecting on her shoulders, breath fogging evenly in the air. The cold registered and passed. No ache followed. No demand.

That, more than anything else, told her how close the line was.

She started walking, boots sinking into snow that should have slowed her down and didn't.

The clock wasn't loud. It didn't tick. It just kept moving forward, indifferent to whether she was ready when it ran out.

Amara walked until the anger caught up with her.

It rose the way heat did here—quiet at first, then everywhere at once. In her chest. In her jaw. In the tight way her hands curled inside her sleeves. She cut across the street instead of following the sidewalk, boots punching through drifts that folded back in behind her like they'd never been disturbed.

Every window she passed glowed warm.

Families sat down to dinner. Someone laughed too hard at something on a screen. A dog barked once, lazy, then settled. Life continued with the calm efficiency of people who had already decided this was fine. Better than fine. Good.

She stopped short in front of a house she didn't recognize, breath sharp, pulse finally racing like it should have been all along.

"How are you all okay with this," she said out loud.

Snow filled her mouth when she exhaled again. The words vanished the moment they left her lips.

She tried another house. Then another. Every porch held boots steaming faintly. Every driveway sat cleared down to dark, warm pavement. Someone had left a window cracked open upstairs, winter air spilling uselessly into a room that stayed comfortable anyway.

It felt like screaming into insulation.

She turned the corner and nearly collided with Mrs. Kline from three doors down, bundled halfway out of a parka she carried instead of wore.

"Oh—Amara," the woman said, smiling easily. "You're out late."

"So are you."

Mrs. Kline waved a hand. "Couldn't sleep. Too warm."

The word landed wrong.

"Doesn't that bother you?" Amara asked.

The smile faltered, then reset. "Bother me how?"

"The heat. The snow. The way everything's changing."

Mrs. Kline adjusted the scarf around her neck, more for politeness than need. "Change happens," she said. "At least this one keeps us alive."

"At what cost?"

The woman studied her, eyes kind, tired. "Honey, cost is a luxury question."

She walked on before Amara could respond, boots crunching softly, posture relaxed.

Amara stood there shaking, fury pressing up against her ribs with nowhere to go.

Luxury question.

She started walking again, faster now, passing the community center where lights still burned inside. Through the glass she saw bodies moving, stretching, laughing. Someone wiped condensation from a window with a bare forearm and leaned into the cleared circle to watch the snow fall, fascinated.

No fear. No hesitation. No argument.

She pushed through the door.

Warmth hit her immediately, thick and enclosing. Conversations dipped when she entered, then resumed. Someone waved. Someone offered her tea. The same cup she'd abandoned earlier still sat on the counter, untouched, steam curling gently upward.

"Why does nobody care," she said, louder than she meant to.

A few heads turned.

Mina Park looked up from a clipboard. "Care about what?"

Amara laughed, sharp and humorless. "You're growing citrus in permafrost. Children run outside without coats. People get sick when they leave town. Something under us is rewriting basic biology and you're asking what."

Mina set the clipboard down slowly. "Lower your voice."

"No," Amara said. Her hands shook now, finally betraying her. "You're all acting like this is a gift. Like survival without consent counts as kindness."

A man near the back snorted. "Easy for you to say. You can still leave."

"For now."

That drew attention.

Mina's expression tightened. "You're scaring people."

"They should be scared."

"They're fed," Mina said. "They're warm. They're alive."

Amara stepped back, heat pressing in from every direction. "So was my mother," she said. "Until she wasn't."

Silence spread unevenly. Someone cleared their throat. A child laughed too loudly at a game in the corner.

Mina softened her voice. "You're grieving."

"I'm furious," Amara said. "I'm alone in a town that decided questions are dangerous."

Mina didn't argue. She only said, "You can't force people to want answers."

Amara backed toward the door, chest tight, skin flushed. "Then stop pretending this is choice."

She left before anyone could respond. Outside, the cold met her again and slid away without resistance. Snow struck her face and melted. The ground beneath her feet held steady, patient, supportive.

She stood there, breath coming fast now, anger burning hotter than the vents beneath the street.

Being the only one who saw the problem didn't make her brave.

It made her isolated.

The feeling settled deeper than the cold ever had. It pressed inward, quiet and heavy, until even the sound of her own breathing seemed far away. Amara stood on the sidewalk with snow brushing her coat, streetlights glowing amber through the fall, the town moving around her with gentle indifference.

She took a step.

Then another.

At some point, the street changed.

She realized it only because the houses no longer matched the ones she remembered passing. Different porches. Different fences. A mailbox painted blue instead of white. Her boots stood half-buried in snow that looked freshly fallen, smooth and untouched.

Amara stopped.

The streetlamp above her flickered once, then steadied. Snow drifted through its light in perfect lines. Her breath fogged the air, slow and even.

She searched her memory for the last clear moment—leaving the community center, anger sharp in her chest, the door swinging shut behind her.

After that, the sequence blurred.

She checked her phone. The screen lit up, brighter than expected. The time made her frown. She swiped, then swiped again, as if the numbers might rearrange themselves into something familiar.

"How long," she murmured.

The word felt strange in her mouth.

She looked down at her hands. Snow clung to her sleeves, half-melted, darkening the fabric. Her fingers stayed steady. No ache. No stiffness.

The skin felt warm, almost flushed, as if she'd been indoors recently.

A laugh drifted from somewhere nearby. Amara turned toward it and found a small group of people standing at the corner—neighbors, she thought, though their faces took a moment to place. Someone passed around a mug. Steam lifted from it in lazy curls.

"Amara!" a man called. "You heading home?"

She hesitated. The answer should have come easily.

"Yeah," she said, after a beat that stretched longer than it should have. "I think so."

He nodded, satisfied, already turning back to the conversation. No concern. No curiosity.

She walked on, pulse quickening now, awareness sharpening around the edges. Her route corrected itself without conscious effort. Left here. Right there. Her body remembered even when her mind struggled to keep pace.

When her mother's house came into view, relief hit hard enough to make her dizzy.

The porch light glowed steady. Snow gathered along the steps, half-melted, half-frozen again. She climbed them slowly, each step grounding her a little more.

Inside, the warmth wrapped around her instantly.

She leaned back against the door and closed her eyes, counting her breaths until the room settled. The house held steady. The clock on the wall ticked softly, its sound almost startling after the quiet outside.

Amara opened her eyes and looked at it.

She had no memory of walking the last two blocks.

The realization slid into place without drama, without panic. Just a quiet, unsettling certainty.

Time, it seemed, had moved on without waiting for her.

# A Single Thought

Amara returned to her mother's house and went straight to the attic.

She'd avoided it since arriving—too full of dust and memories and things that her mother had saved for reasons only she understood. But if there were answers anywhere, they'd be there.

The attic was cramped, insulated poorly, and cold compared to the rest of the house. Boxes lined the walls, stacked haphazardly, labeled in her mother's careful handwriting.

**AMARA - CHILDHOOD**

**TAXES - 2010-2015**

**PHOTOS - FAMILY**

And at the back, covered with a sheet, three boxes labeled simply: **PERSONAL.**

Amara pulled them out and carried them downstairs, setting them on the kitchen table under better light.

The first box contained more journals—twenty years' worth, continuing where the notebook from the archives had left off.

She opened the most recent one and started reading.

*January 8th. Amara called today. She sounded tired. Distant. I wanted to tell her not to come back. But how do you tell your daughter that her home is no longer safe for people like us? People who remember what cold used to feel like?*

*January 15th. The heating bill is unsustainable. I know this. But every degree I turn it down, I feel the town creeping in. Changing me. I need the heat to remember who I was.*

*January 29th. I saw Tunde today. He's a good man. He's built something remarkable here. But he's not the boy I remember. That boy questioned things. Pushed back. This man has made peace with something he shouldn't have accepted.*

*February 1st. The children frighten me. Not because they're cruel, but because they're content. They don't question why they can play outside in subzero temperatures. They don't wonder why the ground is warm or why older buildings have symbols carved into their foundations—warnings from people like James Mercer who saw what was happening and tried to resist.*

*They don't question because questioning feels unnecessary when you're comfortable.*

*That's how it works. That's how it's always worked.*

*First, it makes you comfortable. Then it makes you compliant. Then it makes you dependent.*

*And by the time you realize what you've lost, you need it too much to leave.*

Amara turned pages, hands shaking.

*February 8th. I'm colder all the time now. Dr. Cruz says my body is rejecting the adaptation process. He says some people's physiology can't integrate the changes, and those people face a choice: leave or die.*

*But leaving isn't really an option, is it? I've lived here for fifty-six years. This is my home. My husband is buried here. My memories are here.*

*I won't be driven out by something that doesn't even know I exist.*

*February 10th. I know what will happen. My body will keep fighting. The cold will keep seeping in. And eventually, I'll simply stop being warm enough to continue.*

*It won't be violent. It won't even hurt much.*

*I'll just... stop.*

*And the town will call it exposure. Natural causes. An old woman who couldn't adapt.*

*They won't call it resistance. They won't call it refusal.*

*But that's what it is.*

*February 12th. I'm ready. I've said my goodbyes in the ways I can. I've left the records where someone might find them. Amara, if you're reading this—and I think you will be—don't make the choices I made.*

*Don't let principle kill you.*

*The organism isn't wrong for doing what it does. It's just biology. Survival doesn't have morality.*

*But humans do.*

*And that means we get to choose how we face extinction. Do we change ourselves beyond recognition to persist? Or do we remain ourselves and accept that some endings are inevitable?*

*I've made my choice.*

*You'll have to make yours.*

*Whatever you choose, know that I love you. Know that I'm proud of you. Know that resistance can be survival too—just of a different kind.*

The entry ended there.

Amara sat at the kitchen table, the house hushed around her, her mother's journal spread open beneath her hands. The pages blurred as tears slid down her cheeks, darkening the paper where they fell. She wiped at her face and kept reading anyway, breath hitching, chest tight, as the familiar handwriting cut straight through her.

Her mother had seen it early. The pattern. The shape of what was happening beneath the town and inside its people. The way warmth crept upward and bodies followed. The way staying changed you, quietly and completely.

And she had chosen resistance.

Every line in the journal carried intention. Careful observations. Dates circled. Margins crowded with questions that sharpened instead of softened over time. This wasn't confusion or denial. It was conviction, held steady even as the cost grew heavier.

Some things mattered more than endurance. Some lines, once crossed, erased meaning itself.

Amara swallowed hard, the words pressing into her ribs as if they'd been written there too.

She pushed the journal aside and reached for the second box. The cardboard creaked softly as she opened it. Inside, folders lay stacked with meticulous order, their edges worn from handling. Weather logs filled the first stack—decades of temperatures plotted into unwavering lines, each winter colder than the last. Charts followed, showing births, departures, the slow reshaping of the town's population into something younger, hardier, quieter.

Beneath those sat medical files. Redacted names. Familiar measurements. Notes written in clinical shorthand that still managed to feel personal. Bone density trending upward. Metabolic rates adjusting. Heat tolerance increasing across generations.

Amara's throat tightened as she turned page after page.

This hadn't been a suspicion. It had been a case. Built patiently. Protected fiercely. A record assembled with the knowledge that understanding wouldn't stop what was coming—but silence might slow it long enough for someone else to choose differently.

She closed the folder and reached for the final box.

It held a single envelope.

Her name lay across the front in her mother's careful script. The paper had been folded, unfolded, then sealed again, as if the decision to write it had taken time to settle.

**Open when you're ready to decide.**

Amara stared at the words until they steadied. Her hands shook as she slid a finger beneath the seal and pulled it free. The paper inside was thin, creased once down the center.

She unfolded it and began to read.

*My dear Amara,*

*If this letter has found your hands, then I have already gone ahead. And if you are reading it, I know exactly where you are standing—at the same crossroad that once held my feet still.*

*I cannot choose for you. A mother has no such right. This decision belongs to the one who must live inside it.*

*But let me tell you what I came to understand.*

*What lives beneath that town does its work without anger. It does not chase, it does not threaten. It moves the way the earth always has—slow, sure, and uninterested in our fear. What took ages before, it now does quickly. Years instead of lifetimes.*

*That is why your choice still matters, even when it feels small.*

*You can leave. Even now. Even if your body has begun to answer the warmth before your mind does. Leaving will hurt. It will feel like swimming against a current that knows your name. But discomfort is still a kind of freedom.*

*You can stay. You can let yourself change. You can become what the town quietly asks its people to be. You will live. You may even find peace there, in time.*

*Or you can do what I did.*

*You can hold the line. You can insist on yourself—your breath, your limits, your definition of what it means to be human. You can keep the heat high and refuse the ease being offered. Know this, my daughter: the body is patient, but biology does not bargain. The cost of staying yourself may be heavy. It may be everything.*

*None of these paths are foolish. None of them are soft.*

*They are simply yours.*

*That thing beneath the ground will take much—comfort, certainty, the future you once pictured so clearly. But it cannot take your will all at once. It cannot choose for you while you are still here.*

*So choose, Amara.*

*Choose with your eyes open. Choose with the same care you use when you listen before you speak. Choose the way your name deserves.*

*And remember this, always: whatever you decide, you were loved by a woman who made her choice with full awareness and an unbroken heart.*

*Nọrọnụ nke ọma,*

*Mama*

Amara folded the letter along its original crease, slow and deliberate, pressing the paper flat with the heel of her hand as if smoothing it might keep the words from echoing. The envelope lay open beside her, its torn edge uneven, final.

She didn't move after that.

The kitchen sat around her in a held breath. The overhead light hummed softly, steady and warm. A pot she hadn't used rested on the stove, clean, untouched. Her mother's mug still waited near the sink, a faint ring of tea darkened into the ceramic like a bruise that never healed.

Outside the window, snow slid down the glass in narrow trails before vanishing. More followed. Always more.

Amara stared at the tabletop until the grain blurred. Her hands rested there, palms down, fingers splayed as if grounding herself to something solid. They looked like her hands. They felt like her hands. Warm. Capable. Wrong in a way she couldn't articulate without breaking apart.

A sound left her before she realized it had formed.

It wasn't a sob. It wasn't a cry.

It was small. Thin. A sharp intake of breath that caught halfway and refused to go further.

Her shoulders folded inward. She leaned forward, forehead hovering inches above the table, breath coming uneven now. The letter slid slightly beneath her elbow. She pressed it back into place without looking, a reflex born of years watching her mother protect paper from careless movement.

"Mama," she whispered.

The word cracked open something she'd been bracing shut since the funeral. Since the bench. Since the ground beneath the town had answered questions her mother had asked out loud for decades.

Her chest seized, tight and burning, and suddenly the air felt insufficient. She pushed back from the table and stood too quickly, chair legs shrieking against tile. The sound rang through the house, sharp and intrusive, then faded.

The silence rushed in to fill the space it left.

Amara pressed her hand to her sternum and paced the length of the kitchen. Her steps felt uneven now, rhythm gone. She crossed to the window and leaned her forehead against the glass. Cold met her skin, registered, released.

"I don't want this," she said, the words shaking loose. "I don't want any of this."

Her reflection stared back at her, faint and doubled by the falling snow. Her eyes were red-rimmed. Her mouth trembled, then firmed, as if muscle memory refused to let her fall apart completely.

She slid down until she sat on the floor, back against the cabinet, knees drawn to her chest. The tile seeped chill through her jeans, a contrast sharp enough to sting. She welcomed it.

Memories surged without invitation.

Her mother at the stove, hair wrapped in a scarf, humming off-key while chopping onions with practiced speed. Her mother at the table late at night, glasses slipping down her nose as she wrote and rewrote the same sentence. Her mother standing at the thermostat, jaw set, turning it higher while the rest of the house slept.

"You don't need to suffer," Amara had said once, annoyed, half-asleep.

Her mother had smiled without looking at her. "I need to feel."

The grief hit fully then.

It came heavy and fast, a wave that knocked the air from her lungs. Amara doubled over, arms locking around her legs as a sob tore free, loud and unrestrained. Another followed. Then another. Each one dragged something loose from deep inside her, something she'd been holding tight with both hands.

Tears soaked into her sleeves. Her nose burned. Her throat ached. She rocked back and forth on the tile, small movements that did nothing to stop the pain but made it survivable.

"She tried," Amara choked. "You tried."

The house gave no answer.

She pressed her face into her knees and cried until her body shook, until her breath hitched and stuttered, until the sound softened into something hoarse and broken. Time stretched and warped around her, minutes dissolving into an indistinct blur.

At some point, she became aware of the heat again.

It pressed gently at her back, steady and constant. The cabinets were warm. The floor beneath her legs radiated faint comfort. The house held her without asking.

That made it worse.

Anger flared through the grief, sharp and sudden. She slapped her palm against the tile, the sound flat and useless.

"You don't get to make this easy," she said aloud, voice raw. "You don't get to take her and then make it easy."

Her breath shuddered. Tears kept coming, slower now, heavier.

She dragged herself upright and staggered to her feet. Her legs felt unsteady, as if she'd been crying for hours instead of—she glanced at the clock—forty minutes.

Forty minutes.

The number sat wrong in her head.

She wiped her face with the hem of her shirt and crossed the kitchen, moving on instinct. Her mother's bedroom door stood open. She hadn't gone in there since the funeral.

The air inside felt different. Still warm, still held, but quieter somehow, as if the room itself knew it was waiting.

Amara stood in the doorway for a long moment before stepping inside.

The bed was neatly made. Her mother's scarf lay folded at the foot, the fabric worn soft from years of use. The dresser held the same careful arrangement of items it always had: lotion, comb, notebook, pen. Everything in its place.

Amara crossed the room and picked up the comb.

Her hands shook again.

She pressed the comb to her chest and slid down onto the edge of the bed. The mattress dipped beneath her weight, familiar. She bent forward, shoulders collapsing, and this time the sob that broke free tore through her completely.

"I don't know how to do this without you," she cried. "You were supposed to tell me what to do."

Her voice cracked into silence.

She lay back on the bed and stared at the ceiling, tears sliding into her hair. The heat wrapped around her, persistent, undeniable. Beneath the house, beneath the town, something continued its slow, patient work.

Amara closed her eyes, and let her grief wash through her fully, no longer fighting it, no longer bracing. It hurt. It burned. It carved something raw and permanent into her chest.

In the space where her mother should have been, Amara lay trembling, heart breaking open wide enough to finally feel the weight of what had been lost—and what she would have to carry alone.

# Heat Soaked

Amara found Tunde in the subterranean corridor, seventy feet below the surface, inspecting a junction where three tunnels met.

He looked up as she approached, no surprise on his face. "I figured you'd come eventually."

"We need to talk."

"About?"

"Everything. The organism. The town. The choices you've made." She stopped a few feet away from him. "How long have you really known?"

Tunde set down his clipboard and leaned against the warm concrete wall. "Five years. Maybe longer if I'm being honest. I had suspicions before that, but five years ago, I stopped being able to pretend they were just suspicions."

"And you kept building. Kept digging deeper. Kept bringing people closer to it."

"I kept keeping people alive. Yeah."

"By changing them."

"By giving them a chance." His voice was measured, calm. "Amara, do you know what the projection is for this region in the next twenty years? Thirty? The climate models are catastrophic. Winters that make this look temperate. Summers that don't come at all. Agricultural collapse. Infrastructure failure. Mass migration that has nowhere to go because everywhere else is collapsing too."

"So, your solution is to let an alien organism remake humanity?"

"My solution is to not let everyone I care about die when they don't have to."

Amara started pacing the tunnel. "You don't get to make that choice for them."

"Someone has to make it. That's what leadership is. Making the impossible choices so other people don't have to carry them."

"That's not leadership. That's tyranny dressed up as paternalism."

Tunde's jaw tightened. "You think I wanted this? You think I sleep well knowing what's under this town? Knowing what it's doing to all of us?" He pushed off the wall. "I have nightmares, Amara. Every night. I dream about the moment when someone figures out what's happening and decides to destroy it. To 'save' humanity. And in those dreams, I watch every child in Grayhaven die as their bodies realize they can't regulate temperature anymore. I watch Isaac Reed collapse in his own backyard because his physiology was built for symbiosis and someone took that away."

"So, you're keeping it secret to protect them."

"I'm keeping it secret because telling the truth doesn't save anyone. It just makes the horror visible without offering solutions."

"Information is a solution. Knowledge is a solution. People have a right to—"

"To what? To choose?" Tunde laughed bitterly. "The people here *are* choosing. Every day. They choose to stay. They choose to have children. They choose to build lives here. Just because they don't know the exact mechanism doesn't mean they don't understand the trade."

"They can't consent to something they don't fully understand."

"No one fully understands anything, Amara. You think people outside this town understand the ecological collapse they're contributing to? The systems that are killing the planet? They don't. But they keep participating because the alternative is harder than the complicity."

Amara stopped pacing. "That's different."

"Is it?"

"Yes. Because climate change is a result of collective human action. This is something being *done to us* by a non-human entity."

"And the organism is here because something—maybe natural selection, maybe deliberate engineering—put it here to ensure life continues. Is that worse than humans destroying themselves through ignorance and greed?"

They stared at each other in the warm tunnel.

"You've really made peace with this," Amara said quietly. "Haven't you?"

"No. I've made a choice. Peace is something else entirely."

"What choice?"

"To prioritize the living over the principle. To accept survival even if it comes at the cost of purity. To build something that lasts even if it's not what I'd have chosen." He met her eyes. "What choice are you making?"

"I don't know yet."

"You're running out of time."

"I know."

"Do you?" He pulled out his phone and showed her a photo. Isaac Reed, playing in the snow. Mina Park, standing with a group of students. A woman Amara didn't recognize, holding a baby bundled in light blankets. "These people are alive because of what the organism does. They're healthy. They're thriving. That baby was born two months premature and should've needed intensive care. Instead, she was home in three days. Perfect cardiovascular function. Perfect temperature regulation."

"Because she's not human anymore."

"Because she's *adapted.* Because she's what humanity might need to be to survive what's coming."

"And what if what's coming never comes? What if this is all preparation for a future that doesn't happen?"

"Then we built a town full of people who can survive impossible cold and we never needed to use that gift. I'll take that outcome over the alternative."

Amara looked down the tunnel, toward the deeper levels where the warmth was more pronounced. "The organism is accelerating. Cruz thinks it's transitioning to a new phase. That the cold will intensify soon."

"I know."

"And you're okay with that?"

"I'm *ready* for that. We've reinforced the deep structures. Expanded the greenhouse capacity. Stockpiled supplies. When it comes—when surface temperatures become uninhabitable for unadapted humans—Grayhaven will be the only place for a thousand miles where people can survive."

"People who aren't people anymore."

"People who are alive. Which is more than can be said for everyone who insisted on staying 'pure.'" He moved closer to her. "Your mother fought this. You know what it cost her. Is that really what you want?"

"My mother died herself."

"My mother died because she stayed herself. There's a difference."

The words hung between them.

"You think I'm a coward," Tunde said finally. "For accepting this. For not fighting."

"I think you're scared. I think you've rationalized capitulation as pragmatism."

"And I think you're privileged. You got to leave. You got to spend seven years out there, studying ice, feeling like you were part of the solution. You don't know what it's like to stay in a place that's dying and watch people choose between slow death and fast death and there's no third option."

"There's always a third option."

"Name it."

"Resistance. Documentation. Warning people what's coming so they can prepare on their own terms."

"I've run those scenarios. You know what happens? Panic. Governments intervene. They quarantine the town or they try to weaponize the organism or they try to destroy it. And in every single scenario, people die. Lots of people. Probably everyone here."

"So, you choose silence."

"I choose survival. For as many as I can save." He picked up his clipboard. "I know you don't agree. I know you think I'm wrong. But when the cold comes—when it really comes—you'll understand. Survival isn't pretty. It's not noble. It's just... continuing. That's all. And sometimes that's enough."

He walked past her, down the tunnel toward the surface.

Amara paused in the corridor, heat soaking through the walls and into her bones, steady and persuasive. The air carried a faint mineral tang, the smell of stone warmed from the inside out. Pipes whispered behind the panels, a low circulation that felt less mechanical than habitual, as if the building itself had learned how to breathe.

She understood Tunde then. The understanding arrived without forgiveness or absolution, just clarity. He had stood where she stood now and weighed bodies against ideals, futures against numbers. He had chosen the path that kept lungs filling and hearts beating, even as the definition of living shifted inch by inch. He had chosen continuity over purity, warmth over doubt.

Her chest tightened with the weight of it.

She could see the logic. She could even respect it. What she could not do was follow it.

Somewhere between endurance and integrity, between adjusting and remaining, there had to be room to stand without being pushed by heat or terror. A place where the body did not dictate the terms of belief. A place her mother had claimed with quiet stubbornness and paid for in full.

Amara stood there, caught at that same edge, wondering whether that kind of resolve was bravery or a slower, quieter way to disappear.

She turned and started toward the stairs.

With every step upward, the warmth loosened its hold. The air thinned, sharpened. Her skin prickled as temperatures shifted, sensation returning in small, precise signals. By the time she reached the exit, her breath came visible again, pale clouds blooming and fading in front of her face.

Outside, snow poured down in dense sheets, heavier than before. The digital display across the street glowed through the fall: −20°F, the numbers flickering as if preparing to drop again. Wind cut through the lot, carrying a cold that pressed hard and fast, demanding attention.

The transition had begun.

She felt it in the way the snow struck the ground and stayed intact, in the way the air bit deeper with every inhale. Beneath her feet, far below concrete and steel, the source continued its work, shifting conditions with patient certainty.

Soon the town would feel it fully. Soon every household would face the same calculation Tunde had already made, the same narrowing corridor of options.

Amara stood in the snowfall, pulse steady, fingers tingling as sensation sharpened. The cold challenged her body, asked questions the warmth never did.

She reached into her coat and pulled out her phone.

Her thumb moved through her contacts, past familiar names, past numbers tied to a life that felt increasingly distant, until it stopped. A climate research station. Northern latitude. Long winters. People who studied cold instead of fleeing it.

Her thumb hovered above the screen, the glass cold beneath her skin. Snow settled into her hair and along her collar, melting slowly, leaving damp trails she could feel but barely register. Wind pressed in harder now, cutting across the open lot, tugging at her coat with insistence. Behind her, warmth lingered—close enough to sense, patient enough to wait.

Amara stood in the middle of it, breath even, heart steady, the decision balanced on the smallest motion.

One call would open the door to voices that spoke in models and projections, people who measured catastrophe in data sets and probabilities. They would ask for proof. They would ask for access. They would arrive with equipment and urgency and certainty. And whatever lived beneath Grayhaven would be dragged into the light, torn apart, or sealed off in ways that left no room for the people above it to survive.

She pictured streets emptied overnight. Homes abandoned mid-meal. Children like Isaac coughing and overheating as the town's protection vanished beneath their feet.

Her grip tightened on the phone.

Silence carried its own weight. Staying meant allowing the transformation to continue unchecked, bodies reshaped quietly, generation by generation, until leaving became impossible and the idea of anywhere else faded into abstraction. It meant living inside a future chosen by something ancient and indifferent, a future that kept people alive while asking them to surrender pieces of themselves without ceremony.

Her pulse kicked harder then, a rare flare of resistance.

The screen dimmed. Then went dark entirely.

Amara let her hand fall. She slid the phone back into her pocket and turned away from the open lot, from the boundary she could still cross, from the call she almost made.

Her boots carried her toward her mother's house without hesitation. The path felt familiar, practiced, even as her thoughts churned.

The decision hovered just out of reach, unformed but pressing. She felt it gathering, tightening the space around her, demanding clarity she didn't yet possess.

She wasn't ready.

The town wasn't ready.

The thought followed her all the way back to the house, settling heavier with every step. Lights glowed behind curtains. Doors closed softly. Somewhere a radio played low, muffled by insulation and warmth. Grayhaven slept the way a body slept under anesthesia—kept alive by systems humming beneath the surface.

Amara shut the door behind her and leaned against it, letting the click of the latch echo through the entryway. The house answered with heat, familiar now, almost comforting. That realization stirred something sharp and unwelcome.

She pushed away from the door and moved through the rooms without turning on lights. The house knew its shape. So did she. Her hand brushed the back of a chair. The edge of the counter. Each surface held warmth like a held breath.

In her mother's bedroom, the window remained cracked open, just enough to let cold spill in. The curtain stirred faintly. Amara crossed the room and stood in the narrow band of chill, letting it cut across her face and arms. Her skin prickled, then adjusted.

Too quickly.

She closed the window.

In the living room, the clock read later than she expected. She frowned, tried to reconstruct the evening. Municipal building. Corridor. Snow. The phone. The walk home. The pieces lined up, but the spacing between them felt wrong, stretched thin like fabric pulled too far.

She sat on the couch and pressed her palms into the cushions. Warm. Everything warm.

A quiet anger stirred again, slower this time, more deliberate.

"You're making it easy," she said to the empty room.

The house did not argue.

She reached for her laptop instead.

The screen bloomed to life, light sharp in the dim room. Her fingers moved on instinct, pulling up old folders, research notes she hadn't opened since Norway. Climate models. Permafrost studies. Adaptation thresholds. She skimmed quickly, eyes snagging on familiar terms.

Cold shock. Thermal tolerance. Metabolic shift.

Her breath slowed as something clicked into place—not a solution, but a shape.

Grayhaven wasn't an endpoint.

It was a trial run.

The thought landed hard enough to make her sit back. The organism beneath the town didn't feel reactive. It felt preparatory. As if this place had been selected. Isolated. Contained. Cold enough to matter, small enough to manage.

She imagined other towns like this one, scattered across latitudes, waking quietly into warmth while the world beyond them froze. She imagined borders hardening, survival clustering around pockets of adaptation.

Humanity, divided by temperature.

Her stomach twisted.

A sound outside pulled her attention to the window. Movement across the street. Someone out late. She recognized the shape after a moment—Isaac's father, coat slung over one arm, keys dangling from his fingers. He paused on the sidewalk, looking up at the sky as snow collected on his hair. He didn't hurry inside.

Amara watched him for a long moment.

He wasn't afraid.

The realization brought an unexpected grief with it. Fear had vanished here. Fear had been engineered out of the equation, replaced with warmth and continuity and the promise of survival.

But fear was also a warning.

She closed the laptop slowly.

Her mother's notebook sat on the table where she'd left it. Amara picked it up and flipped past the familiar pages until she reached the back. Blank paper waited there, untouched.

She took a pen from the drawer.

Her hand hovered, then moved.

**Date.**

**Time.**

**Location.**

She paused, then added a new line beneath it.

**Subject:** *self.*

The word made her pulse quicken.

She wrote carefully, describing the cold outside, the way it registered and passed, the moment earlier when time had slipped sideways without permission. She noted the warmth in the house, the ease of movement, the absence of discomfort.

Her handwriting stayed steady.

If no one else was ready, she would be. She would watch herself the way her mother had watched the town. Measure. Record. Refuse to let the changes go unnamed.

Amara set the pen down and closed the notebook. She stood at the window and met her reflection again, eyes clear despite everything.

If the town wasn't ready, she would become something else entirely—a witness.

# Acceleration

The cold arrived in the night without ceremony.

Amara surfaced from sleep into a stillness so complete it felt dense, as if the air itself had thickened. The house held its breath. No pipes shifting. No distant wind. Even the usual settling sounds were gone, swallowed whole.

She sat up slowly, pulse already climbing.

Her phone lay on the nightstand, screen dark. When she picked it up, the glass felt sharp against her fingers. The display bloomed to life.

−32°F.

Her jaw tightened.

Yesterday's number flickered through her mind, then the one before that, the steady downward slide accelerating past anything that felt gradual. The margin for adjustment had vanished overnight.

She swung her legs out of bed and stood, floorboards warm beneath her feet, heat pushing upward from below with practiced efficiency. The contrast made her dizzy. She layered clothing with quick, economical movements—thermal fabric hugging skin, fleece trapping warmth, insulated pants stiff with bulk, sweaters pulled tight, coat heavy enough to drag at her shoulders.

By the time she reached the door, her hands were already trembling—not from cold, but from anticipation.

She opened it.

The air struck her full in the chest.

It drove the breath from her lungs in a sharp, involuntary gasp, a force that felt solid, almost edged. The world beyond the threshold looked unchanged—snow piled high, sky pale and empty—but the sensation cut deeper than sight. Her breath burst into glittering vapor the instant it left her mouth. Moisture gathered at the corners of her eyes and crystallized before she could blink it away.

Each inhale burned. Each exhale scraped.

She stepped onto the porch. The wood beneath her boots groaned faintly, sound snapping off short instead of carrying. Her skin tightened everywhere at once, a full-body recoil. Even with warmth threaded through her muscles, even with the quiet recalibration she'd felt taking hold over days, this cold demanded attention.

She forced herself down the steps.

Snow screamed under her boots, dry and brittle. The driveway stretched ahead, a clean white plane reflecting light without softness. Steam curled faintly from the ground near the foundation, rising straight up before vanishing.

By the time she reached the end of the drive, her vision had narrowed. Her chest felt wrapped in wire. Her body struggled to decide which signals mattered most.

Enough.

She turned back, boots slipping once before finding purchase, and moved fast. The door slammed shut behind her, sealing the cold outside with a violence that echoed through the house.

Warmth surged to meet her.

She crossed the living room on unsteady legs and twisted the thermostat higher. The vents answered immediately, a rush of heated air rolling across her skin. She sank onto the couch, elbows braced on her knees, teeth chattering as sensation rushed back too fast.

Her hands ached. Her face throbbed. Her breath came shallow and quick.

This was different.

She leaned back and closed her eyes, focusing on the heat pouring into her, letting it soak deep enough to loosen the tight band around her ribs. Slowly, the shaking eased.

If this cold had pushed her back inside within seconds, she didn't need imagination to picture what it was doing elsewhere. She saw bare hands fumbling with keys. Elderly neighbors pausing too long at doors. Children whose bodies still ran cooler, faster, fragile in ways the town preferred not to think about.

The house held steady around her, warmth climbing higher, compensating without question.

She brought the phone to her ear and listened to it ring once.

"I know," Cruz said, his voice already tight. "I was waiting for this call."

Behind his words, she caught the layered sounds of the clinic—metal trays shifting, hurried footsteps, a door swinging open and shut too hard.

"How bad is it?" she asked.

"I've had four come in since dawn." Papers rustled. "Hands. Feet. Ears. People who've lived here thirty, forty years. People who should have walked through this without trouble."

Amara pressed her fingers into the couch cushion. Warm. Still warm. "What's changed."

"The pull," he said. "It's stronger. Deeper. The heat draw isn't steady anymore—it's accelerating." He paused, then added quietly, "My projections didn't account for this pace."

Her stomach tightened. "Give me a number."

A breath on the other end. Measured. Controlled. "If the curve holds… we could hit sixty below before the week's out."

The room seemed to tilt. "That's—"

"—beyond endurance," Cruz finished. "Yes."

She closed her eyes. "Who makes it."

"The kids," he said immediately. "Anyone born into this system. Their baselines are different." His voice dropped. "The rest of us are balancing on a narrowing edge."

"Can the body finish the change?" she asked. "Can it catch up?"

"Possibly." He hesitated. "If people stay alive long enough. If warmth stays accessible. If the transition doesn't outrun us."

Silence stretched between them, filled with the low murmur of the clinic.

"I need to see it," Amara said finally. "I need to see what this looks like outside."

"Cover everything," Cruz replied. "Skin exposure is a liability now. Minutes matter."

She ended the call and stood, already reaching for her coat. This time she layered without hesitation—another sweater pulled tight, thermal leggings under insulated pants, scarf wound high across her mouth and nose until her breath warmed itself before escaping. Goggles pressed against her face, sealing out the air.

When she stepped outside, the cold met her like resistance.

It pushed back.

The street had changed. Snow lay harder, its surface crusted and sharp, light reflecting off it without softness. Each step rang louder, brittle sound snapping off short. The air scraped against her scarf, found gaps anyway, stung at her cheeks.

The town had gone quiet in a way she hadn't known was possible.

A figure crossed the street ahead of her, head down, movement brisk and economical. Another hurried from one doorway to the next, keys fumbling with stiff fingers. Doors opened and closed quickly, heat spilling out in brief, visible waves before sealing again.

No one lingered.

No one waved.

The benches sat empty. The paths children had carved through snow the day before had vanished under fresh accumulation. Even the community center windows glowed dimmer, curtains drawn tight.

Amara moved carefully, counting her breaths, aware of time in a way she hadn't been days ago. The cold pressed in from all sides, insistent now, testing limits.

The streets had emptied.

Amara realized it only after she'd walked three blocks without hearing a single voice. No shrieks cutting through the cold. No boots skidding. No children racing ahead of one another with hats dangling from sleeves they refused to wear. The absence pressed harder than the temperature.

She stopped in front of the school.

The doors stood shut, their metal frames rimed with frost despite the heat that still pulsed beneath the building. A paper sign had been taped to the glass, the corners already curling from condensation and cold.

**ALL CLASSES MOVED TO SUBTERRANEAN LEVELS**
**UNTIL FURTHER NOTICE**

The words looked temporary. They felt permanent.

She turned toward the community center. Its windows were dark now, curtains drawn tight. The place that had once glowed late into the night—

games, voices, steam-fogged glass—sat sealed and quiet, as if it had pulled inward to survive.

The clinic told a different story.

A line stretched down the sidewalk, bodies layered until they lost individual shape. Scarves wrapped high. Hoods pulled low. Goggles clouded at the edges. People shifted from foot to foot, conserving heat, breath pluming in short, controlled bursts. No one spoke.

Amara didn't stop.

Her feet carried her toward the square without conscious decision. Toward the open space where Isaac Reed had crouched in the snow, hands bare, shaping walls with careless confidence.

The castle still stood.

Half of it, anyway. One turret slumped inward, softened by fresh snowfall. The steps he'd carved had vanished, smoothed flat as if they'd never existed. Snow crept up the sides steadily, reclaiming the structure grain by grain.

Amara stood there longer than she should have, cold biting through her layers, eyes fixed on the ruin.

She pictured Isaac's grin. The way he'd talked about happiness like it was something simple. Contained. She imagined him now, deep underground where the heat held steady, lungs filling easily, body perfectly tuned to what the town was becoming.

Safe.

"You won't find them up here."

The voice came from behind her, muffled and close.

Amara turned. Mina Park stood a few feet away, bundled so thoroughly that only her eyes showed, dark and glossy behind the rim of her hood.

"It's getting bad," Mina said.

"Yeah," Amara replied.

Mina shifted her weight, boots crunching sharply. "I stepped outside to check the locks. Two minutes." She shook her head slightly. "My face went numb before I reached the corner."

Amara glanced at her cheeks, already flushed beneath the fabric. "Your body's trying to catch up."

Mina's eyes flicked to hers. "And if it doesn't?"

The wind slid between them, sharp and dry.

Amara stayed quiet.

Mina let out a breath that fogged thickly. "Right." She adjusted her scarf higher. "I should get back in."

"Wait," Amara said, stepping closer. Heat rose faintly through the ground beneath them, steady as a pulse. "Are you scared?"

Mina laughed once, short and brittle. "Terrified." Her voice softened. "But also stuck."

She gestured at the buildings around them, their windows glowing faintly through layers of frost. "I don't have anywhere else. My job's here. My students. My apartment. I can't just leave and start over."

"Even if staying costs you everything?"

Mina's gaze dropped to the snow, to the half-buried castle. "Out there," she said, nodding toward the unseen edge of town, "it costs you slowly. Here, at least, there's warmth. People. Something holding us together."

She looked up again, eyes tired but resolute. "That has to count for something."

Then she turned and hurried toward the nearest building, the door opening just long enough to spill a wash of heat before sealing shut again.

Amara stayed where she was as the square emptied around her, snow thickening until it blurred the edges of everything familiar. The castle Isaac had built collapsed inward, its walls losing shape beneath the weight of fresh accumulation, the careful angles erased without effort. Snow no longer fell in clean lines. It came slanted, erratic, driven by gusts that scraped across the open space and stung exposed skin.

Across the square, a door burst open. Warm light spilled out in a harsh rectangle before snapping shut again as Tunde crossed the distance toward her, boots cutting fast, direct paths through the drifts.

"You need to get inside," he said, breath sharp, words clipped.

"I'm fine," she replied, though her jaw felt stiff and her tongue thick.

He didn't argue. His hand closed around her arm, firm, urgent, and steered her toward the municipal building. Snow clung to his coat, already melting. The door opened, and heat slammed into her face with such force it made her gasp. Her skin burned as circulation surged back, pins and fire racing across her cheeks and nose.

She staggered once, catching herself on the wall. "How bad is it?" she asked.

Tunde yanked off his gloves, shoved them into a pocket. His hands looked steady. Capable. Pinked by heat rather than cold.

"Worse than projections," he said. "We're clearing the surface. No more temporary shelter. Everyone goes down. Permanently."

Her stomach dropped.

"The deep levels are holding," he continued, already walking. "Seventy feet down, it's stable. Warm enough to sleep without layers. The systems are solid."

She followed him into the lobby, where voices overlapped and footsteps echoed from corridors beyond sight. The air smelled of damp wool, sweat, and metal heated too quickly.

"We'll survive," he added.

She stopped walking. "As what?"

He turned, impatience flaring across his face. "As whatever keeps breathing."

"Tunde—"

"I don't have room for this," he cut in. His voice rose, sharp enough to slice through the background noise. "I have families lining the halls. I have kids crying because their pets froze before anyone could bring them inside. I have elders who can barely move fast enough before the cold locks their joints." His chest heaved once before he forced it down. "I need to move two hundred people underground before nightfall."

He gestured toward the unseen corridors. "Down there, they'll live."

"And up here?"

He didn't answer immediately.

"What about the ones who didn't change fast enough?" Amara pressed.

Tunde's mouth tightened. "We keep them warm as long as we can."

"And when that stops working?"

His eyes flicked away. When they came back, something brittle had settled into place. "Then biology decides."

Her voice dropped. "So, they die."

"They face reality," he said. "The same one your mother faced."

The words hit like a slap.

"She chose a line," he went on, quieter now, harsher for it. "So did everyone else who thought refusing the process would stop it. Evolution doesn't pause because someone disagrees."

He turned away from her and started issuing orders, his voice snapping into authority as people responded from somewhere below. Doors opened. Equipment clattered. The building shifted into motion, heat redistributing, systems adjusting.

Amara stood alone in the center of the lobby.

Warmth pressed against her from every surface, relentless and enclosing. The walls radiated it. The floor held it. Even the air carried it heavy and thick in her lungs.

She understood then that this moment—this compression of time and temperature and choice—marked the end of hesitation. The organism beneath them had crossed from preparation into execution.

It was awake now.

It had begun to move with intent.

The pressure showed first in the air. The way it pressed closer to the skin, thickened the breath. The way the building's systems worked harder, vents sighing more often, heat cycling faster as if trying to keep pace with something accelerating beneath them.

Amara stood near the lobby windows and watched the numbers on the exterior display drop again. Then again. Each change arrived quicker than the last, the digits blinking as if unsure they could keep up.

Her body responded before her thoughts did. A subtle tightening in her chest. A faint ache along her jaw. Sensations she recognized now as thresholds—signals that the margin was shrinking.

She pressed her palm to the glass. Cold radiated through it in sharp clarity. It registered. It passed. Too quickly.

Twenty-four hours, her mind supplied, not as a calculation but as a weight.

The corridors around her filled with movement. Families streamed past carrying bags hastily packed. Someone dragged a rolling suitcase that rattled loudly against the floor. A woman argued with a security volunteer, her voice strained, breaking on a child's name. Somewhere deeper inside the building, a door slammed and stayed shut.

No one looked up.

The town had entered a kind of forward momentum that did not allow for witnesses.

Amara drifted back toward the exit, then stopped. Warmth wrapped her again, persuasive and immediate. Her skin relaxed under it without effort. The ease scared her more than the cold ever had.

She stepped outside once more.

The storm swallowed her instantly. Snow fell thick and fast, driven sideways now, stinging against her goggles. Wind pushed at her shoulders, demanded balance. The square had vanished into white motion, the outlines of buildings reduced to vague shadows.

She moved carefully, counting steps, letting the cold bite deep enough to matter. Her breath came harder this time. The warmth inside her resisted the loss, fought to maintain itself.

That resistance felt new.

It felt trained.

She reached the center of the square and stopped, snow already gathering along her boots. Somewhere beneath her feet, far below stone and concrete and earth, the pulse had changed. Faster now. Stronger. The rhythm carried urgency, as if the thing below had reached the final stretch of its long work.

It no longer felt patient.

It felt focused.

Amara closed her eyes and pictured the road beyond town, the invisible line where the snow thinned and the air shifted. She pictured her car, the engine turning over, the first miles feeling wrong but tolerable. She pictured heat that didn't come from below, warmth that didn't ask for anything in return.

Then another image rose unbidden: Isaac's calm smile. The school sign taped to frozen glass. Children descending underground with backpacks and blankets, their bodies already prepared for what waited ahead.

Refuge, the town would call it.

Survival.

She opened her eyes as wind tore at her coat. Her fingers tingled now, sensation sharpening rather than fading. The cold demanded more from her than it had hours ago.

The clock was tightening.

Grayhaven shifted around her, pulling inward, reshaping itself into something singular and sealed. A place built to cradle those who could change fast enough. For everyone else—

Amara turned slowly, snow sweeping around her legs, and faced the storm head-on.

# Outside World

Amara barricaded herself in her mother's house and opened her laptop.

If she was going to warn someone—anyone—it had to be now. Before the cold made leaving impossible. Before her adaptation locked in completely.

She pulled up her contacts list. Scientists she'd worked with. Colleagues from research stations. University professors who specialized in climate systems and extremophile biology.

She started typing an email:

*Subject: Urgent - Unexplained Physiological Changes in Northern Population*

*I'm writing from Grayhaven, a small town in [coordinates]. Over the past decade, residents here have undergone rapid adaptive changes that appear to be linked to an unknown organism beneath the town. Changes include extreme cold tolerance, altered metabolism, and generational acceleration of these traits in newborns.*

*Current situation is deteriorating rapidly. Surface temperatures dropping beyond normal seasonal patterns. Population showing signs of symbiotic dependence on the organism.*

*I have documentation. Medical records. Historical data. This needs immediate investigation.*

Her thumb lingered above the screen, the cursor blinking like it was breathing.

The draft sat there, heavy with implication. A few more words and it would be out of her hands—forwarded, archived, escalated. She could already imagine the replies arriving with polite urgency, the questions sharpening, the machinery beginning to turn.

People would come.

They always did.

They would arrive with insulated cases and careful language, with credentials and contingency plans. They would walk the corridors and look down into the heat and call it unprecedented. They would talk about containment and risk and necessary losses.

And the losses would have faces.

Mina's tired smile. Isaac's easy certainty. The infant Tunde had shown her weeks ago, swaddled and warm, breathing without effort in a world that would soon kill anyone like him beyond the snowline.

Her jaw tightened.

She hit delete, and the words vanished. The empty field stared back at her, neutral and patient.

She started again.

*Subject: Climate Research Opportunity*

Her fingers moved faster now, steadier. The language stayed clean. Technical. Familiar.

*Unusual meteorological patterns observed in northern region. Localized cooling exceeding current models. Potential relevance to feedback loops and regional tipping points.*

She paused, then added one more line.

*Data available upon request.*

It sounded like a conference abstract. Something that could sit quietly in an inbox without setting off alarms.

She sent it to three names she trusted—people who asked questions before making calls.

The sent confirmation blinked once, then disappeared.

Her chest loosened just enough to notice the ache beneath it.

She opened a new window and pulled up the state emergency contact page. The cursor hovered again, this time over a phone number. She imagined the conversation unfolding in clipped exchanges.

*>Temperatures dropping rapidly.*

*>>Yes, ma'am, we're aware of the cold front.*

*>People at risk.*

*>>Please advise residents to remain indoors.*

She pictured trying to push past that, trying to explain what lay under the town, how warmth rose from the ground like breath, how bodies were changing in response. She saw the pause on the other end of the line, the careful shift in tone, the suggestion of evaluation rather than action.

Her hand fell away from the mouse.

She closed the laptop.

The room settled around her, heat pressing in from the walls, the floor, the air itself. Somewhere beneath the house, the steady pulse continued, faster now, intent clear in its rhythm.

Official paths required names and proof and certainty. She had none of those she could afford to give. Tunde had been right about that.

The realization tasted bitter, but it held.

Amara sat back in her chair and stared at the darkened screen, knowing she had just chosen the narrowest possible line—one that delayed destruction without guaranteeing rescue.

Her phone rang, sharp and sudden in the quiet room. An unfamiliar number lit the screen.

She answered on the second ring. "Hello?"

"Ms. Okoye? This is Dr. Sarah Chen. I'm calling about your message."

Amara straightened, pulse kicking hard enough to feel in her throat. "You got it."

"I did," Chen said. Papers shifted faintly in the background, the low hum of an office somewhere far away. "You mentioned anomalous cooling. I've been collecting similar reports from northern regions. Small communities. Isolated infrastructure."

Amara closed her eyes for half a second. "So I'm not the only one."

"No," Chen said carefully. "You're one of several."

Hope flared, quick and dangerous.

"The temperatures here are dropping faster than projections allow," Amara said. "Daily. Hourly, in some cases. And the people—" She stopped, recalibrated. "Their bodies are responding in ways I've never seen."

"How so?"

"Increased cold tolerance. Circulatory changes. Children born here show baseline differences from adults who moved in." She paced as she spoke, bare feet warm against the floor. "It's coordinated. Accelerated."

There was a pause on the other end. Longer this time.

"That kind of change takes generations," Chen said. "Even under extreme pressure."

"I'm aware."

"Then you understand why I'm struggling with this."

Amara stopped pacing. "I'm standing in the middle of it."

Chen exhaled softly. "Human systems don't rewrite themselves this fast."

"Something is helping them."

"That's a conclusion, not an observation."

"It's both," Amara said, sharper now. "I can feel it. I can measure it. I can watch it happen."

Another pause. Keyboard clicks. A distant voice muffled by a door.

"What exactly are you suggesting?" Chen asked.

"I don't have language for it yet," Amara said. "But it's localized. Persistent. And it's changing the conditions for survival."

Chen's tone cooled, professionalism tightening into place. "If you have datasets—continuous temperature logs, physiological records, anything peer-reviewable—I can look at them. Without that, I can't justify mobilizing resources."

"By the time you finish reviewing," Amara said, "people here will be past the point of leaving."

"That's true in many cold regions."

"They can't relocate," Amara said.

"Everyone can relocate."

Her grip tightened around the phone. "Their bodies won't tolerate it."

Silence.

"That's a serious claim," Chen said finally.

"So is what's happening here."

"I can make a note," Chen said. "Flag the region for continued monitoring."

"That won't stop this."

"I don't have authority beyond that," Chen replied. "If conditions worsen, local emergency services—"

"They're already overwhelmed."

"I'm sorry," Chen said, and meant it in the distant way people did when distance kept them safe. "If you obtain verifiable evidence, contact me again."

"People are dying," Amara said.

"People die every winter," Chen replied gently. "Encourage precautions. Minimize exposure."

The line clicked.

Amara lowered the phone slowly, staring at the dark screen until her reflection surfaced faintly against it. Her face looked flushed. Warm. Steady.

She let the phone fall onto the couch beside her.

The room felt smaller now. The air thicker.

She stood there for a long moment, listening to the heat move through the house, to the quiet certainty beneath it all.

Someone had listened. It just hadn't been enough.

Amara sat alone at the kitchen table, the house wrapped tight around her, heat pressing from every surface. The quiet felt deliberate, the kind that followed after doors closed and decisions were quietly made elsewhere. She understood then why her mother's warnings had stayed inside these walls.

Every truth her mother had uncovered carried the wrong shape. It asked listeners to accept something that sounded impossible, something that bent language until it resembled panic. And the thing beneath Grayhaven had done its work carefully, threading itself through bodies and habits until separating it from the town would mean tearing people apart along with it.

She picked up her phone again.

The first call went to her former professor. The man answered with familiarity, his voice warm in a distant, academic way.

"Amara," he said, surprised. "It's been a while."

She spoke quickly, careful, choosing words that might land. Temperature curves. Physiological shifts. A closed system behaving like an incubator.

There was a pause, then a soft sigh. "Send me whatever you have," he said. "I'll look. You know how extraordinary this sounds."

"I do."

Another pause, longer this time. "Be careful," he added, already retreating into caution.

The second call rang longer. When the journalist answered, her tone came bright, curious.

"This better be good," she said lightly.

Amara laid it out again, tighter this time. Cold. Isolation. Bodies responding in ways that shouldn't exist yet.

The interest held until one word shifted the balance.

Underneath.

There was a laugh on the other end of the line, sharp and disbelieving. "That's a wild pitch," the woman said. "I'd read it for fun, but I can't run it. I need something I can put my name on."

Amara ended the call without arguing.

The phone rested in her palm, heavy and inert. The screen reflected her face faintly—eyes too bright, skin flushed by warmth that never asked permission.

No one was coming.

She stood and crossed the room, boots still by the door, dusted with snow that had already melted into the mat. Outside the window, the digital display across the street flickered again.

−38°F.

The number barely registered before it changed.

Her laptop chimed softly. One new message.

She opened it.

Thanks for thinking of me, but I'm buried in Antarctic work right now. If you find anything publishable, send it along. Otherwise—stay warm!

Her mouth twisted.

Stay warm.

As if warmth were neutral. As if it didn't arrive with conditions. As if it didn't ask for pieces of you in exchange.

She closed the laptop and stood in the center of the room, breathing slowly, feeling the house respond. Heat rose from the floor. The walls held it. The air stayed thick and gentle in her lungs.

This was where her mother had stood, night after night, turning the dial higher, insisting on sensation even as it exhausted her. This was where she had chosen to resist with small, daily acts, holding the line until her body failed before her will did.

Amara pressed her palms together, then let them fall apart.

She didn't know whether that choice had been bravery or simply refusal carried to its end.

What she did know was that the window was closing.

If she left, it had to be now—before the cold sharpened further, before her body learned too much, before the road beyond Grayhaven stopped accepting her.

Amara reached for her coat.

The cold was still falling.

Amara felt it in the way the house worked harder around her—vents cycling more often, a low, constant push of heat that pressed against her skin like a hand refusing to let go. Outside the window, snow streaked past faster now, driven sideways by a wind that scraped along the siding and worried at the seams.

She didn't wait for the numbers to change again.

Upstairs, the hallway felt narrower than it had an hour ago. Warmth pooled along the floorboards, clung to the walls, followed her step for step. She moved quickly, opening drawers, pulling clothes free with practiced efficiency. Thick socks. Thermal layers. Anything that might buy her time once she crossed the line where the snow thinned and the air shifted.

Her hands hesitated only once—at the closet door.

Inside, her mother's coat still hung where she'd left it, wool worn smooth at the elbows, pockets heavy with forgotten things. Amara pressed her face briefly into the fabric, breathed in the faint trace of soap and something older, something uniquely hers. Then she slid it from the hanger and folded it carefully into the bag.

Documents went next. Passport. ID. Papers her mother had insisted she keep in one place. The journals followed, their weight grounding, solid. Proof of a life lived deliberately.

She zipped the bag and stood still for a moment, listening.

The house answered with heat.

Her body answered too—heart steady, breath even, muscles loose and cooperative. It felt ready in a way that frightened her more than exhaustion ever had.

Downstairs, she paused at the bottom of the steps. The front door waited, a clean rectangle of wood and metal separating her from the storm. Snow rattled softly against the glass, persistent, impatient.

She imagined the drive ahead. The road narrowed by drifts. The headlights carving a tunnel through white. Mile by mile, the temperature shifting. Her body protesting, recalibrating, struggling to remember how cold was supposed to feel when it wasn't cushioned by something rising from beneath the ground.

Her grip tightened on the bag strap.

Staying would be easier. The town offered that without shame. Warmth without effort. Survival without movement. A future shaped quietly, efficiently, until leaving became unthinkable.

Outside, the wind howled harder, a long sound that slid along the eaves and vanished.

Amara stepped into her boots. The rubber soles were warm.

She opened the door.

Cold slammed into her, sharp and immediate, stealing breath and balance in one motion. Snow struck her face, found the gaps in her scarf, burned against her cheeks. She welcomed it. Let it hurt. Let it demand something of her again.

She stepped onto the porch and pulled the door shut behind her.

For a heartbeat, she stood there, snow gathering on her shoulders, wind tugging at her coat, the house's warmth sealed away inside. The town lay ahead, buried and glowing faintly beneath the storm, already turning inward.

This was the line.

She took one step down. Then another.

Her body flinched, then steadied.

She walked toward her car, each breath scraping, each movement deliberate. The organism beneath the town continued its work without pause, indifferent to direction or defiance.

Amara tightened her grip on the bag and kept going.

A sound cut through the storm.

It wasn't wind. It wasn't the scrape of snow against siding or the distant groan of stressed metal. This sound carried shape—too sharp, too human. A shout, torn thin by the cold, then swallowed again.

She stopped.

The square lay half-visible through the whiteout, streetlamps reduced to blurred halos. For a moment there was nothing else. Then the sound came again—closer this time. Panic edged it, raw and unsteady.

"Help—!"

Amara turned toward it without thinking, boots skidding as she fought the wind. The cold bit hard now, punished the hesitation. Her breath burned. Good. She leaned into it.

Near the corner of the square, a figure stumbled into view. An older man, bundled poorly, one glove gone, the other hanging uselessly from his sleeve. His face shone red and wet beneath frost. He took two steps and fell hard to one knee, hands slapping uselessly at the snow.

Amara reached him as he tried to stand again and failed.

"Easy," she said, grabbing his arm. The heat under her palm startled her—too much, too fast. His skin felt wrong, flushed and slick despite the air stealing warmth from everything else.

"I just—" he gasped. "I was going to the clinic."

His words tangled together. His pupils looked blown wide behind ice-crusted lashes.

"How long have you been outside?" she asked.

He shook his head weakly. "Didn't think it'd be this bad."

She knew that look. Cruz had described it. Bodies caught between states. Heat regulation spiraling. The cold outside, the pull beneath, both demanding something his system couldn't decide how to give.

She hauled him upright with effort and half-dragged him toward the nearest building. Each step took more from him. His weight sagged heavier against her shoulder, breath stuttering.

A door burst open ahead of them. Light and warmth spilled out. Someone shouted for help. Hands reached out, pulled him from her grip, carried him inside.

Amara stood there, snow plastered to her coat, chest heaving.

The door slammed shut.

The warmth vanished instantly, sealed away.

She stared at the door for a long second, then looked down at her hands. They were steady. Responsive. Her pulse slowed with deliberate efficiency, as if her body had already logged the emergency and moved on.

That terrified her.

Because she remembered the last time she'd tried to leave.

Years ago. Just after her mother's first collapse. A planned trip. A suitcase by the door. The car loaded. She'd made it three miles past the boundary before nausea hit like a wall, heat flooding her veins until she'd had to pull over, gasping, vision tunneling. Her mother had waited in the passenger seat, silent, watching, knowing.

They'd turned back together.

That time, it had been about her mother.

This time, it was about everyone else.

The man she'd helped would live—for now—because someone had dragged him inside. Because the town still had enough warmth to rescue its own. But that window was narrowing. She could feel it. The storm carried urgency now, the cold pressing harder, faster.

Soon there would be too many of them.

And she would be one more body choosing warmth over movement. One more person standing at the threshold telling herself she still had time.

Amara looked back toward her car. Snow had already begun to cover the tracks she'd made. The town was erasing hesitation as efficiently as it erased footsteps.

If she stayed longer, the choice would be made for her again.

She adjusted the strap of her bag, turned her back on the square, and broke into a run.

# Just Five Minutes

Amara worked by feel more than sight, the dark thick with her own breath. Each exhale burst into the air and hung there, a pale cloud that refused to drift away, turning the space around her car into a shifting fog. Frost gathered instantly along her lashes. Snow squealed under her boots with every step, dry and brittle, a sound that snapped short instead of carrying.

The number on her phone glared back at her before the screen dimmed again.

−42°F.

The cold cut through layers with surgical precision. Gloves slowed her fingers to useless paddles. The scarf across her face trapped moisture that froze against her skin, pulling tight with every breath. Air scraped down her throat, sharp enough to make her chest seize, each inhale a deliberate act instead of instinct.

She hauled the bag into the back seat and slammed the door harder than she meant to, the sound echoing too loud in the empty street. The driver's door resisted for a heartbeat before giving way. She slid inside and turned the key.

The engine coughed, then caught.

The heater blasted air that felt almost insulting in its weakness. Lukewarm at best. She wrapped her hands around the steering wheel, feeling vibration slowly creep into her palms as the car protested the cold. Minutes stretched. The engine temperature crawled upward by degrees that felt theoretical rather than real.

Five minutes. Ten.

Her breath steadied. Sensation crept back into her fingers in painful sparks. She shifted into gear and eased forward, tires chewing into drifts that had reshaped the street into rolling contours.

The road no longer resembled a road. Snow lay in ridges and valleys, the suggestion of pavement buried beneath. She followed memory more than markings, correcting gently when the car drifted, refusing to rush.

There were no headlights ahead. No taillights behind.

Grayhaven had folded inward.

Houses loomed half-submerged, roofs heavy with snow, porches erased. Windows sat dark at street level, while faint amber glows leaked from basement windows, low and constant, like embers buried under ash. Life had retreated downward, clustering around warmth that rose from beneath the ground.

She passed the community center, its doors sealed, its windows black. Passed the clinic, where a dim strip of light marked the entrance below street level. Passed the school, its playground buried, swings frozen in place, classrooms relocated deep where children breathed easily.

The town square opened up around her, a wide white expanse where the snow castle had vanished entirely, smoothed flat as if it had never existed. Wind swept across it unchecked, carving patterns that changed even as she watched.

She drove through the center of it, heart pounding harder now, awareness sharp and bright.

The municipal building slid past on her right, its lower windows glowing steadily. Orders were being given down there. Decisions finalized. Lives reorganized around depth instead of distance.

Her grip tightened on the wheel.

At the far end of town, the sign emerged from the snow, letters crusted with ice, the town name barely legible beneath accumulation. She slowed as she approached it, the moment stretching thin.

She passed the sign.

The road beyond narrowed immediately. Snow thinned just enough to show darker patches beneath. The air felt different—still brutal, still punishing, but without the subtle upward pressure she'd grown accustomed to. Her body reacted at once. A spike of dizziness. Heat flaring under her skin in confused response.

She drove on anyway.

Behind her, Grayhaven disappeared into the storm, a pocket of engineered warmth sinking deeper into itself.

Ahead, the road unraveled into a pale, endless blur, the horizon erased by wind and falling snow. Amara leaned closer to the wheel as if proximity alone could keep the car anchored to the ground. Each breath scraped through her chest, raw and burning, her eyes stinging until tears slipped free and froze along her lashes.

The road fought her immediately.

Snow lay in heavy drifts that swallowed the tires up to their rims. The engine growled low and angry as she pressed forward, momentum her only ally. Tires spun, caught, spun again, the steering wheel shuddering in her hands as the car clawed its way through uneven ground.

One mile.

The headlights carved tunnels through white, revealing ridges and sudden dips that jerked the car sideways before she corrected. Her shoulders ached with the effort of staying steady.

Two miles.

The snow thinned in patches, less compacted, looser. Wind cut across the road in sharp bursts, pushing flakes sideways instead of straight down.

Three miles.

Her dashboard clock flickered as the car bounced. The temperature display shifted, the number changing almost imperceptibly at first.

Four miles.

–38.

The air felt different against her face, sharper, more abrasive. The steering wheel no longer felt like an extension of her hands but an object she had to consciously hold.

Five miles.

–35.

Her breath came faster now, shallow and strained. She rolled her shoulders once, then again, trying to shake off the tightness creeping up her spine.

Ahead, the snowfall changed texture. The rigid, vertical descent fractured into something messy and alive. Flakes spun, collided, drifted in erratic paths. The boundary announced itself before it appeared.

Six miles.

–28.

Her pulse hammered against her throat.

The line came into view—faint but unmistakable. A seam stitched across the landscape where one kind of sky gave way to another. On one side, snowfall fell with eerie discipline. On the other, winter behaved like winter again.

Seven miles.

–20.

Her body reacted as if struck.

A sharp prickling erupted across her arms and neck, heat flaring beneath her skin. Her hands tightened involuntarily on the wheel, fingers locking as a wave of dizziness rolled through her. The cabin felt suddenly too small, the air too thick.

Her chest seized.

Eight miles.

–15.

The boundary loomed just ahead, close enough to touch. Fifty feet. Less.

Pain tore through her in earnest. Heat surged violently, crawling under her skin like fire trapped beneath ice. Sweat broke out along her hairline despite the cold, soaking into her scarf, making her gasp as warm moisture met freezing air.

Her lungs refused to cooperate, each breath shallow and frantic. The world tilted, headlights smearing into bright streaks.

She slammed the brakes.

The car skidded sideways, tires shrieking before finally stopping, angled toward the invisible line she could no longer approach. The engine idled harshly, vibration rattling through her bones.

Amara bent forward over the wheel, breath hitching, vision narrowing. Heat roared through her veins, unbearable and wrong, every nerve screaming as her body rejected the temperature beyond the boundary.

She pressed her forehead to the steering wheel and fought for air, forcing slow inhales, counting them through clenched teeth.

The boundary waited just ahead.

Her body refused to follow.

Heat surged anyway, rising fast and violent, a pressure building beneath her skin with nowhere to go. Her pulse thudded against her throat, each beat louder than the last. The steering wheel vibrated under her grip as her hands began to shake, fine tremors at first, then sharp enough to rattle her wrists. Her chest tightened, breath coming shallow and uneven, air scraping in without ever feeling sufficient.

Her body was fighting itself.

Blood rushed too fast, too hot, her system reacting as if the air ahead were poison. A wave of dizziness rolled through her, dragging sparks across her vision. Sweat broke out along her spine and pooled beneath her collar despite the brutal cold seeping through the doors.

Twenty feet ahead, winter behaved like winter.

Crossing that line would finish her.

Her mind understood it with brutal clarity. Her body screamed it even louder.

She pressed her forehead to the steering wheel, eyes squeezed shut, counting breaths that refused to slow. The heat inside her felt wrong—aggressive, invasive, a defense mechanism turned inward. Her heart hammered as if trying to outrun her own skin.

The realization landed fully then, heavy and final.

This was what her mother had known.

This was what that last walk into the garden had meant. The quiet certainty. The refusal to keep pretending there was still a way back.

Some changes sealed themselves without ceremony.

Some thresholds announced themselves only after they had been crossed.

She traced the last two weeks backward in her mind—not a single moment, no dramatic instant. A collection of small accommodations. Faster recovery. Less pain. Warmth that lingered longer than it should have. The way the cold had stopped frightening her.

Cells rewriting themselves patiently. Thoughtlessly.

She had crossed over without noticing.

Enough to belong.

Enough to be barred from leaving.

Her hands loosened on the wheel. She swallowed hard, throat burning, and shifted the car into reverse.

As the tires rolled backward, the pain eased. The heat receded from a roar to a throb. Her breathing steadied, lungs finally cooperating as the temperature outside dropped again. The farther she moved from the boundary, the more her body settled, relief spreading with disturbing ease.

The drive back blurred together.

Snow thickened. The disciplined vertical fall returned, flakes descending with mechanical consistency. The car moved more easily now, her muscles unclenching, her pulse slowing as if she were returning to a familiar climate instead of a trap.

The town rose out of the storm gradually, shapes emerging through white. Buildings hunched under accumulation. Streets erased down to corridors of snow. Life pressed underground, announced only by the dim amber glow leaking from basement windows.

Grayhaven welcomed her back without resistance.

She parked in front of her mother's house and let the engine idle, hands resting uselessly in her lap. The house radiated warmth even through the walls, a steady presence she could feel from the curb.

Her throat tightened.

"I tried," she whispered into the empty car.

The words fogged the air and vanished.

Trying had never been the metric. Biology ignored effort. Survival ignored intent. The thing beneath the town had no use for principles.

She turned off the engine and opened the door.

The cold wrapped around her immediately.

−45°F.

Her body accepted it without protest.

No gasp. No panic. Just sensation.

She stepped out, boots sinking into snow that barely registered as cold anymore, and closed the door behind her.

Her body settled into the cold as if it had always belonged there. Heat no longer surged in protest. Blood moved with quiet efficiency. Breath came easy, steady, unremarkable. The air that would have shattered an unaltered body passed through her lungs without resistance, as familiar as a well-worn room.

She crossed the yard toward the front door, boots sinking into snow that barely registered anymore. Each step carried weight. Not pain—something heavier. A slow reckoning. A recognition that the struggle had ended without ceremony, without victory on either side. The fight had simply stopped asking for her input.

Inside, the house greeted her with a wave of warmth that made her flinch.

She moved straight to the thermostat and turned it down.

Seventy pressed against her skin, cloying and intrusive. Her shoulders tightened. She adjusted it again. Sixty. The air softened immediately, settling into something her body could accept.

Amara peeled off her coat, then her sweater, leaving them draped over the back of a chair like discarded skin. She sat on the couch in a t-shirt and jeans, legs tucked beneath her, pulse calm. The room held steady around her, a temperature that once would have demanded blankets and wool and constant vigilance.

Her mother would have been shivering here.

That thought landed quietly and stayed.

The change had finished its work. There were no sharp edges left to it, no remaining resistance to grind down. Her nerves had rewritten their expectations. Her blood had learned a new rhythm. The house felt less like shelter now and more like a compromise.

She reached for her phone.

The draft still waited there—the message she had rewritten a dozen times, the warning sharpened and softened and sharpened again until it barely resembled the truth. She read it once more, thumb hovering, feeling nothing rise in her chest.

Then she deleted it.

The screen cleared, clean and empty.

A new message took its place.

I'm staying. Come find me if you need me. I'll be in the deep levels.

She sent it to Cruz and watched the confirmation appear. One small vibration. One quiet acknowledgment.

Next came the laptop.

She opened folders she knew by heart. Temperature logs. Photos taken with shaking hands. Notes typed late at night while the house breathed heat into her bones. One by one, she erased them. Files vanished. The recycle bin emptied. The screen returned to its blank, indifferent glow.

Evidence dissolved with a few clicks.

It felt final in a way nothing else had.

Warning the world required distance. It required separation. It required a body that could still imagine living somewhere else.

She no longer had that body.

Amara closed the laptop and set it aside. The room felt still, insulated from urgency. Snow slid down the windows in slow sheets. The house ticked softly as it adjusted to the colder setting, pipes settling, walls holding.

She lay back on the couch and let her eyes close.

The cold outside intensified, deepening toward something vast and merciless. She sensed it without fear, without anticipation. Just awareness.

Below the town, beneath foundations and tunnels and centuries of unknowing habitation, the organism continued its work. No thought. No judgment. Only process. Heat drawn inward. Change distributed outward. Preparation carried forward.

Amara breathed in.

Her body answered with quiet efficiency. She had been shaped for this.

Whether she had agreed or resisted no longer mattered.

The thought settled like frost across glass—thin at first, then spreading, branching, claiming surface after surface. Amara lay still on the couch, eyes open, staring at the ceiling where a faint hairline crack traced its way from the corner toward the light fixture. Heat no longer pressed at her skin. The room felt neutral, balanced, a place where her body asked nothing and offered nothing in return.

That was the problem.

She sat up slowly. The house answered with small sounds—wood contracting, pipes adjusting to the lowered temperature. Familiar. Domestic. Safe in the way a cage could be safe if you stopped testing the bars.

Her chest tightened.

Anger came first. Sharp and sudden. It flared without direction, looking for something solid to strike. Her jaw clenched hard enough to ache. Fingertips dug into the couch cushion, nails catching in the fabric. Weeks of questions, of running in narrowing circles, of being the only one in town who still felt the wrongness of it all—compressed into a single, burning pulse.

They had taken her choice.

No. Worse.

They had waited for her body to take it from her.

She pushed herself to her feet and crossed the living room, bare feet sinking into the rug. The floor felt faintly warm beneath her soles, a subtle bleed from below. She paused, then deliberately stepped off the rug onto the hardwood near the door, where the cold seeped up just a little more insistently.

Her skin adjusted instantly.

That made her laugh once—short, brittle, the sound snapping in the air and falling apart before it could become anything else. The laugh scraped her throat raw.

She stopped.

Confusion followed the anger, heavier and harder to shake. It pooled behind her eyes, blurred the edges of the room. She pressed her palm to her sternum as if she might find some remaining human baseline there, some anchor that still reacted the way it used to.

Her heart beat evenly.

Too evenly.

She moved toward the front door. Each step felt deliberate, ceremonial. The coat still hung on the hook by the door, crusted with ice from her return. She took it down and slid her arms into it, the fabric stiff and cold against her skin. No urgency followed. No instinctive recoil.

She wrapped a scarf around her neck and opened the door.

Cold surged in, immediate and forceful. Snow swept across the threshold in fine, dry grains that stung her ankles. The night swallowed the house's light, leaving only the glow from basement windows up and down the street—small, square eyes watching from below ground.

Amara stepped outside and pulled the door shut behind her.

The sound landed dull and final.

The temperature hit her face with blunt force. −45, maybe lower by now. Air that had once stolen breath now slid into her lungs without protest. Her cheeks tingled, then burned faintly, then settled into something close to comfort.

She walked.

Snow squealed underfoot, the sound sharp and brittle. The street lay empty, erased down to contours and shadows. Wind cut across open spaces, lifting snow into twisting sheets that scattered around her legs. Streetlights glowed dimly through ice-fogged halos.

She didn't put on gloves.

Her fingers flushed pink, then steadied. Skin tightened. Sensation sharpened instead of fading. She held her hands out for a moment, palms up, watching fine crystals gather along her knuckles and melt into nothing against her heat.

A marvel, really.

The thought made her stomach twist.

She turned toward the garden.

Her mother's garden lay behind the house, half-buried now, the raised beds lost beneath smooth, unbroken drifts. The bench still sat where it always had, rimmed with snow, the wood dark with moisture and ice.

Amara walked toward it and sat down.

The cold seeped through her coat, through the layers beneath, into her back and thighs. It registered as pressure rather than pain. Her body adjusted again, faster this time, redistributing heat, tightening vessels, conserving without asking her permission.

Tears came then.

They surprised her with their force. One moment her eyes burned, the next her vision fractured as hot tracks spilled down her cheeks.

She didn't wipe them away. She tilted her face up instead, letting the wind catch them.

They froze almost instantly.

Tears turned to ice along her skin, delicate lattices forming where salt and water met air too cold to tolerate delay. Her lashes clumped together, white and crystalline. Her cheeks stiffened, skin pulling tight.

She touched one cheek with a bare finger.

The ice crackled faintly and broke away, falling into her palm like crushed glass.

Her breath hitched.

A sob tore loose then, raw and uncontrolled, the sound ripped from her chest before she could swallow it back. It echoed once against the house and vanished into the night. She bent forward, elbows on her knees, shoulders shaking as another sob followed, then another.

Her mother had sat here.

She could see it too clearly. The set of her shoulders. The way she'd wrapped her cardigan tighter and tighter, as if fabric could hold back what biology had already decided. The way she'd stayed above ground, fighting heat with heat, cold with principle, refusing the easy comfort below.

Amara pressed her forehead into her gloved hands.

"Why didn't you take me with you," she said aloud, the words tearing at her throat as they left her mouth. Her voice sounded strange in the cold, flattened, fragile. "Why didn't you make me leave."

The wind answered by sweeping snow across the garden in a low, hissing wave.

A thought surfaced then, unbidden and terrifying in its clarity.

She could stay here.

She could sit on this bench and let the cold do what it did best. Let exposure stretch time thin. Let her body decide where its limits truly lay. Adaptation had edges. Even now. Even fully altered, there were thresholds she could still cross.

She imagined the heat inside her finally losing the argument. Blood thickening. Systems faltering. The slow, quiet dark that would follow.

Her mother would be there.

That idea slid through her with sickening ease. A reunion carved from frost and resolve. Two bodies refusing in different ways, meeting again in the only place left that felt honest.

Her hands trembled.

She leaned back against the bench, face lifted to the sky. Snow fell harder now, streaking downward in disciplined lines, catching in her hair, building along her shoulders. Her tears continued to form and freeze, layer after fragile layer.

The cold invited her.

Her body answered.

That frightened her more than the thought of dying.

She clenched her fists until her nails bit into her palms, grounding herself in the sting. Breath dragged in and out, each inhale clouding briefly before vanishing. She pictured her mother's face, not at the end, but years earlier—laughing in the kitchen, scolding her in Igbo when she forgot to cover her head, pressing warmth into her hands on winter mornings.

Staying alive meant carrying that memory forward.

Dying here would turn it into an ending.

Amara pushed herself to her feet with a sharp motion, snow cascading off her coat. Her legs felt strong. Too strong. She hated that too.

She brushed ice from her cheeks with the heel of her hand, skin burning faintly as circulation shifted. The tears had stopped. Her face felt rigid, sculpted by cold and resolve in equal measure.

She looked once more at the bench.

"I'm still here," she said to the empty garden. Her voice cracked but held. "Even if I don't know why yet."

Wind swept through the yard again, erasing her footprints almost as soon as she turned away.

Amara walked back toward the house, tears frozen and broken away, anger and confusion braided tight in her chest, carrying both with her into the warmth that no longer felt like comfort—but felt like unfinished business.

# A Human Question

Amara descended into the deep levels.

Not because she wanted to. But because the surface was no longer survivable for anyone, and her body—traitor that it was—needed the warmth that only existed seventy feet below ground.

The corridors were packed now. Families huddled in makeshift living spaces carved out of storage rooms and mechanical alcoves. The community hall had been converted into a dormitory. The school operated in shifts. The greenhouse levels were working overtime to feed a population that could no longer access surface resources.

Grayhaven had become a subterranean city in less than a week.

And everyone was coping with quiet, grim efficiency. Because this was survival. Because adaptation meant accepting new normals. Because questioning used resources better spent on enduring.

Amara found Cruz in the medical bay, tending to an elderly man whose body hadn't adapted fast enough.

"How is he?" she asked.

Cruz looked up, exhaustion carved into his face. "Dying. His cardiovascular system can't handle the stress. He's seventy-three. He adapted slower than most. And now..." He gestured helplessly. "Now it's too late."

The man's breathing was labored. His skin had the waxy pallor of someone whose body was giving up.

"How many?" Amara asked quietly.

"Seventeen dead in the last three days. Another thirty who won't make it through the week." Cruz stripped off his gloves. "All of them older. All of them people who couldn't adapt fast enough when it mattered."

"My mother's cohort."

"Yes."

"And the children?"

"Fine. Thriving, actually. They're treating this like an adventure. Playing in the tunnels. Making up games. They don't remember the surface well enough to miss it."

"What about everyone in between?"

"Surviving. Struggling. Learning that survival isn't the same as living but it's better than the alternative."

Amara sank into a chair. "I tried to leave."

"I know. Tunde told me."

"My body wouldn't let me. I got twenty feet from normal air and I thought I was dying."

"You were dying. Your thermoregulation has been completely rewired. Normal temperatures are toxic to you now. You need the extreme cold to feel okay." He sat beside her. "Welcome to permanent residency."

"Is there any way to reverse it?"

"Maybe. Theoretically. If you spent months in progressively warmer environments, your body might readapt. Might. But the risk of cardiovascular failure during that transition is high. Most people who try to reverse adaptation die in the attempt."

"So, I'm trapped."

"We're all trapped. The question is whether we're trapped alive or trapped dead."

They sat in silence, listening to the elderly man's labored breathing.

"I could still destroy it," Amara said quietly.

Cruz looked at her sharply. "What?"

"The organism. I know where the main mass is. I know it's biological. Biological things can be killed."

"And everyone adapted dies with it."

"Maybe."

"Not maybe. Definitely." Cruz's voice was hard. "I've run the simulations. The children's bodies are completely dependent on the thermal regulation the organism provides. Without it, their cardiovascular systems would fail within hours. Adults who are fully adapted—maybe a week. Partial adaptations like us might survive longer, but we'd face severe physiological distress."

"But humanity would remain human."

"Dead humans are still dead, Amara."

"But at least they'd die themselves."

Cruz stood abruptly. "You sound like your mother."

"Maybe I should."

"Your mother's principles killed her. Is that really what you want? To die for an idea of humanity that doesn't exist anymore anyway?"

"What do you mean?"

"I mean humanity has never been static. We're different from our ancestors ten thousand years ago. A thousand years ago. A hundred years ago. We've always been changing. The only difference now is speed and awareness. We know we're being changed. We feel it happening. But that doesn't make it wrong."

"It makes it involuntary."

"So is every other environmental pressure that shapes species. Gravity. Radiation. Oxygen levels. Predation. Climate. We didn't consent to any of it. We just adapted or died."

"This is different."

"Why? Because the pressure has intent? Because something designed this?" Cruz shook his head. "Intent doesn't matter. Results do. And the result is a population that can survive conditions that would kill everyone else. That's not a curse. It's a gift."

"Even if it cost us our humanity?"

"Define humanity. Seriously. Define it in a way that doesn't include the people sleeping seventy feet underground, raising children, growing food, building community. They're human. They're just not the same humans who walked above ground two centuries ago."

"They're not the same humans who were born to them. That's the difference. My mother gave birth to me before the adaptation accelerated. I had a choice, even if the choice killed me. These children don't. They'll never have a choice. They'll never be able to leave. They'll never know what it means to be human outside this context."

"And that's tragic. I agree. But it's not reason enough to kill them."

The elderly man's breathing stopped.

Cruz moved immediately, checking vitals, attempting resuscitation. But after two minutes, he stopped and pulled a sheet over the body.

"Eighteen," he said quietly.

They sat with the dead man for a moment, giving weight to the passing.

Then Cruz said, "If you destroy the organism, you become a mass murderer. Everyone adapted dies. That's two hundred people, maybe more. Including every child under fifteen. Can you live with that?"

"Can I live with letting it continue? Letting more people be changed without consent? Letting humanity evolve into something unrecognizable?"

"Those aren't equivalents. One is definite death. The other is uncertain change. How is that a fair comparison?"

Amara stood and walked to the small window that looked out into the corridor. People moved past—adapted people, living their adapted lives, making the best of circumstances they hadn't chosen but had learned to accept.

Mina Park walked by, leading a group of students. She looked healthier than she had on the surface. Adapted. Integrated.

Isaac Reed ran past, laughing, chasing another child. Barefoot despite the cold that still leaked down from above.

Tunde appeared, talking to someone about food distribution, his voice calm and authoritative.

All of them alive. All of them adapted. All of them dependent on something they didn't fully understand and couldn't control.

"What would you do?" Amara asked. "If you had the power to destroy it. What would you choose?"

Cruz was quiet for a long time. "I don't know. That's the honest answer. I've thought about it every day for five years and I still don't know. Because both choices end in death. One is fast and definite. The other is slow and uncertain. And I don't know which is more merciful."

"My mother chose slow death."

"Your mother chose for herself. You'd be choosing for everyone."

Amara pressed her forehead against the cold glass. "I miss the surface."

"We all do."

"I miss when choices felt clear."

"They were never clear. We just had less information about how complicated they were."

A siren sounded—three short bursts. The signal for everyone to descend another level. The cold was intensifying again.

People moved calmly, efficiently, deeper into the earth. Toward the warmth. Toward the organism.

Toward the future they'd been prepared for whether they knew it or not.

"I won't destroy it," Amara said finally. "I can't. Not with this many lives dependent on it."

"That's probably wise."

"But I won't celebrate it either. I won't pretend this is anything other than what it is—theft of agency on a scale I can barely comprehend. Survival bought with surrender."

"Survival bought with adaptation. That's all life has ever been."

"Maybe. But that doesn't mean I have to like it."

"No one's asking you to like it. Just to not kill everyone."

Amara left the medical bay and let the door seal behind her with a soft, pneumatic sigh. The air changed almost immediately as she moved deeper into the complex. It grew steadier, heavier, carrying a faint mineral scent that clung to the back of her throat. Heat lingered here in a way it didn't on the surface—distributed evenly, held with intention, as if the walls themselves understood their purpose.

She walked past living quarters first. Narrow hallways opened into clusters of rooms where doors stood ajar. Inside, people lay resting beneath light blankets, faces slack with exhaustion. Some slept curled on their sides, knees drawn close. Others lay flat on their backs, arms flung wide, as though surrendering to gravity. The quiet was dense, punctuated only by the low murmur of ventilation and the occasional cough that echoed too long before dissolving.

Further on, the school rooms came into view. Glass panels revealed children seated at low tables, their voices muted through thick walls. They worked calmly, heads bent over tablets and paper, fingers moving with practiced ease. A teacher paced slowly between them, boots soundless against the padded floor. Jackets hung unused on hooks by the door. A few children had shed their shoes entirely, socks pressed flat against the warm ground.

Amara slowed without meaning to.

One boy laughed suddenly, bright and sharp. The sound pierced her chest and lingered there. Another child leaned over and whispered something, earning a quiet reprimand and a shared grin. Life continued here with startling normalcy, shaped around conditions that would have ended entire cities aboveground.

She moved on.

The greenhouses followed, layered vertically like lungs stacked atop one another. Moist air spilled into the corridor as she passed, fogging the glass briefly before clearing again. Inside, leaves glistened beneath artificial suns. Fruit hung heavy on vines, colors too vivid to feel real. Water trickled along channels cut with precision, feeding roots that pulsed with quiet vigor. Growth thrived here, accelerated and indulgent, as though the earth itself had been persuaded to give more than it ever intended.

Voices drifted out—workers exchanging comments about yield, about schedules, about how quickly the cold had worsened topside. Their tones stayed practical, grounded. Fear rarely survived long in places where routine still functioned.

The corridor narrowed as she descended further. Seventy feet down, the signage changed. Paint faded. Lighting softened into a steady amber glow. The walls here curved more subtly, corners rounded in a way that resisted straight lines. The floor felt faintly resilient beneath her boots, absorbing impact rather than reflecting it.

Warmth settled around her shoulders like a cloak.

She reached the lowest accessible corridor and stopped.

The air here carried a rhythm she felt more than heard. A pressure that rose and fell, slow and deliberate. She lifted her hand and placed her palm against the wall.

The surface responded.

A faint vibration met her skin, steady and deep. Beneath plaster and reinforcement and years of human modification, something immense continued its work. Alive. Enduring. Its presence pressed upward through layers of stone and steel, through soil compacted by generations of footsteps, through a town that had grown dependent without ever fully understanding how.

Her fingers tingled.

The sensation traveled up her arm and settled somewhere behind her sternum, a resonance her body recognized instinctively now. Heat flowed through her veins in response, adjusting, aligning. She closed her eyes.

Images flickered unbidden: early settlers huddled against an unforgiving winter, hands cracking, lungs burning. Fires burning low. Children crying through the night. Then warmth discovered, inexplicable and miraculous, bleeding up from the ground. Survival secured. Gratitude blooming. Structures built. Foundations poured. Homes raised directly atop the source of their deliverance.

No one had meant for this.

Intent rarely mattered to systems older and larger than the people who encountered them.

Her breath slowed as she listened—to the hum of power conduits, to the distant movement of air, to the pulse beneath her palm that never hurried and never paused. Continuity lived here. Preparation. A mechanism set into motion long before Grayhaven had a name, responding to shifts in the planet with quiet inevitability.

Her body stood within that response now.

Cells carried instructions rewritten to favor endurance over fragility. Blood moved differently through her, prioritizing conservation, resilience. Pain had recalibrated its thresholds. Comfort had shifted its meaning.

She opened her eyes.

The corridor stretched ahead, curving gently out of sight. Behind her, life thrived in chambers warmed by borrowed heat. Above her, the surface surrendered to cold that no longer asked permission.

She withdrew her hand from the wall.

The absence of vibration felt immediate, like stepping out of water and into air that lacked resistance. Her skin cooled slightly, though the warmth lingered beneath it, embedded deeper than surface sensation.

She turned and began the walk back toward the living levels.

Each step felt measured. Deliberate. Survival here required movement forward, never back. The complex encouraged that, guiding bodies along paths optimized for function and flow. She passed the greenhouses again, catching the scent of citrus and damp soil. Passed the school rooms, where lessons continued uninterrupted. Passed the sleeping quarters, where dreams unfolded beneath steady ceilings.

No one questioned this place anymore.

Acceptance had become infrastructure.

As she climbed, her thoughts drifted to what had been lost. The easy assumption that humanity stood apart from its environment. The belief that adaptation belonged to the distant past or speculative future. The comfort of imagining choice as something external forces could never fully erase.

She carried those memories like contraband.

Someone had to.

The elevator doors opened ahead, ready to carry her upward. She paused before entering, turning once more toward the depths below. Toward the unseen mass that had reshaped everything quietly, efficiently.

She would survive here. Her body had already made that clear. Endurance would come easily now. Comfort would follow, then belonging.

Yet memory resisted assimilation.

She stepped into the elevator.

As the doors slid closed and the ascent began, Amara fixed her gaze on her reflection in the polished metal wall. Her face looked calm. Capable. Changed. Eyes steady, skin clear, breath unlabored.

She memorized it.

Witnessing mattered. Even if no one else asked for the account. Even if the future required silence as the price of persistence.

She would endure, and she would remember. Somewhere between those two truths, she would carry the last echo of a humanity that once believed survival meant more than adaptation.

# Thorough Endurance

Spring arrived the way everything did down here—without ceremony, without evidence, without asking anyone to notice.

The lights shifted, imperceptibly warmer in tone. Meal rotations adjusted by a few minutes. Sleep cycles stretched, then compressed again. Somewhere in the upper tunnels, a technician changed a setting and the air took on the faintest suggestion of damp earth instead of clean metal. That was how seasons worked now. Through systems. Through schedules. Through subtle permissions granted by people who hadn't seen the sky in a long time.

Amara stopped trying to track it.

Days folded into one another until they lost their edges. Morning meant the low chime that signaled breakfast service. Night meant the lights dimming to their artificial dusk. Her body adapted to that rhythm easily, settling into cycles measured by hunger and fatigue instead of sunrise and shadow.

She marked time by smaller things.

The way her hands no longer stiffened when she touched cold metal railings. The way her breath stayed even after climbing four levels of stairs. The way silence no longer felt temporary.

She hadn't gone back to the surface since the last attempt. Neither had anyone else. Access points remained sealed, monitored only by instruments that relayed data no one debated anymore. The numbers came in steady and merciless, and the discussions they sparked ended quickly.

Too cold.

Too deep.

Too final.

Grayhaven moved inward.

The town reorganized itself around depth instead of direction. Corridors filled with life—voices, footsteps, the clatter of carts rolling over reinforced floors. Living quarters expanded, walls pushed back inch by inch as families claimed space and settled into permanence. Names were painted on doors now. Small decorations appeared: children's drawings taped to bulkheads, plants coaxed into surviving under grow-lights, strings of lights woven through handrails for reasons no one bothered to explain.

People made homes where they could.

Amara passed them daily on her way to the archives.

The air there carried a different weight. Drier. Cooler. The hum of servers layered beneath the deeper pulse she felt more than heard. She liked it here. Or tolerated it better than most places. The archives asked for attention, not participation.

She sat at the long central table, light pooling over paper and screens, and worked.

Her mother's journals lay open beside Cruz's annotated files, their margins crowded with different hands, different fears. Pages smelled faintly of old ink and disinfectant. She traced lines of handwriting she knew by heart now, recognizing the moments where urgency sharpened the script, where exhaustion dragged it thin.

Some days she cross-referenced construction logs with temperature shifts, following the town's expansion downward in parallel with the cold's advance above. Other days she read birth records, noting dates, weights, measurements that drifted further from baseline with each passing year.

Patterns emerged. Then solidified.

She recorded them without commentary.

The population registry blinked on the wall display behind her, updating automatically. The number held steady. It always did. When it changed, it did so cleanly—one life exchanged for another, as precise as a ledger balanced by design.

She didn't linger on the names.

Her work drew quiet attention. People nodded when they passed her table. Some offered updates without being asked. Others avoided her gaze entirely, as if documentation itself carried risk. She understood both reactions.

Witnessing unsettled systems built on acceptance.

She worked anyway.

When her eyes tired, she rested them on the wall and felt the faint vibration through the soles of her boots. The organism's presence threaded through everything here—through heat exchangers, water circulation, the subtle buoyancy in the air that made long days bearable.

It did its work continuously. Without pause. Without deviation.

Children's laughter echoed down the corridor outside the archive door, high and unguarded. Their footsteps moved differently than adult ones—lighter, faster, unburdened by memory of what had been lost. They had never known wind on their faces or the ache of real cold in their bones. This place was their world, complete and sufficient.

Amara closed her notebook and set her pen down.

She flexed her fingers. Steady. Warm.

Somewhere deep inside her, a quiet anger stirred—not sharp enough to burn, not loud enough to demand action. Just present. Persistent. A reminder that adaptation carried a cost even when it succeeded.

She stood and gathered her materials, sliding them into labeled drawers that now filled an entire wall. Records grew daily. So did the need for them.

Someone, someday, would want to know how this happened.

How a town learned to live underground. How bodies learned to endure what the surface could not. How survival reshaped meaning itself.

Amara turned off the desk light and stepped back into the corridor, joining the steady flow of people moving between meals and rest and work.

Time flowed on without markers, and she kept walking with it, carrying the record forward.

She wrote:

*Day 89 below ground.*

*The children are thriving. They've stopped asking about the surface. For them, this is normal. This is the only world that matters. They play in the tunnels. They learn in underground classrooms. They grow up never seeing sunlight and don't seem to miss it.*

*The adults cope. Some better than others. Mina Park teaches with the same dedication she showed on the surface. Tunde manages infrastructure with exhausting competence. Cruz continues his research, documenting the changes none of us can stop.*

*And I write. I record. I witness.*

*I don't know who this is for. No one outside Grayhaven will ever read it. And the people here don't want to. They've chosen survival over memory, which is probably wise.*

*But someone should remember when we were different. When humanity meant something other than this.*

*Even if that memory is all I have left.*

She closed the journal and let her hand rest on the cover a moment longer than necessary, fingertips lingering on the worn edge. Then she stood and followed the corridor down toward the greenhouse level, the air growing wetter with each step. Moisture beaded faintly along the walls here, catching the light and sliding downward in thin, slow tracks. The warmth was gentler than in the living quarters—diffused, cultivated, meant to be absorbed by leaves instead of skin.

The greenhouse doors slid open with a sigh, releasing a breath of green.

The smell hit her first. Loam and chlorophyll, a sweetness that carried memory with it—late summers, open markets, hands stained with juice. Rows of plants stretched out beneath the lights, dense and orderly, leaves broad and glossy, stems thick with health. Water trickled through narrow channels cut into the floor, the sound soft and constant.

Lila knelt between two raised beds, sleeves rolled up, hands buried to the wrist in dark soil. Her hair was pulled back loosely, curls escaping and clinging to her temples. She looked up as Amara approached, a smear of dirt across her cheek.

"You're just in time," Lila said. Her voice carried ease here, a looseness Amara rarely heard anywhere else. "They're ready."

"How are they?" Amara asked, though the answer was already visible in the heavy clusters hanging from the vines.

Lila smiled and rose, brushing her hands together. "Perfect. Better than perfect."

She twisted a tomato free with practiced care and placed it in Amara's palm. It felt warm. Alive with it.

Amara turned it once, thumb pressing lightly into the skin, then bit down. The flesh split cleanly. Juice flooded her mouth, bright and rich, sweetness layered with something deeper, almost savory. She closed her eyes without meaning to.

"That tastes..." The word failed her. She swallowed. "That tastes like it remembers something."

Lila laughed softly. "Right? Like it knows what it's supposed to be."

"How?" Amara asked. The question escaped before she could soften it.

Lila's smile lingered, then shifted into something more uncertain. She looked around the greenhouse, at the vines climbing their frames, at the leaves stretching toward artificial suns. "I stopped trying to explain it. The soil feels different. The roots grow faster, stronger. Maybe the heat carries more than warmth. Maybe we do." She shrugged. "Or maybe we're all tangled up together now in ways my instruments can't catch."

She gestured down the rows. "This shouldn't exist. And yet."

"Here we are," Amara said.

Lila nodded, accepting the words without comment, and turned back to her plants. Amara lingered another moment, watching her work—how careful her hands were, how reverent. Growth had a way of inviting devotion.

Then Amara left the greenhouse and continued downward.

The corridors narrowed as she descended, the lights dimming to a deeper amber. Her footsteps echoed less here, absorbed by surfaces that gave instead of resisted. The air pressed closer to her skin, warmer, heavier, threaded with that familiar rhythm she felt through her bones.

The sealed stairwell waited at the end of the hall.

She keyed in the code Cruz had given her. The lock disengaged with a muted click, and the door swung inward.

Warmth surged out, immediate and enveloping.

The chamber opened before her, vast enough to swallow sound. The ceiling arched high overhead, ribbed and curved, catching the light in soft gradients. The floor gleamed faintly, smooth and yielding, responding to her weight with subtle resilience.

And at the center of it all, the organism rose.

It filled more of the space now, its bulk expanded, its surface alive with motion. Light rippled across it in slow waves—pale gold deepening to amber, then sliding back again.

Patterns traced themselves along its body, repeating and diverging, intricate without intention.

Amara stood still, letting her eyes adjust, letting the heat settle into her muscles.

"It's bigger," she said aloud, the sound vanishing quickly. Or maybe it was only more awake.

She took a few steps forward. The air shimmered faintly around the organism, distortion bending light at the edges. With each pulse, warmth radiated outward, brushing her skin like breath.

"I hate you," she said.

The words landed flat, swallowed by the space. She tried again, louder. "I hate what you did to us. I hate what you're still doing."

The organism continued its steady rhythm, untroubled.

She felt anger rise then, hot and sharp, cutting through the passive acceptance that clung to everything down here. Her hands curled into fists at her sides.

"I hate that my body listens to you," she went on. "That everyone's does. That you made survival feel like a bargain we didn't even get to read."

She moved closer, close enough now to feel the heat intensify, close enough that the vibration beneath her feet aligned with her pulse. Her chest tightened.

"I hate that leaving hurts," she said, voice breaking despite herself. "That staying feels easier every day. That comfort came wrapped around something that cost us the right to say no."

She stopped just short of touching it.

The light along the organism's surface brightened, then dimmed again. No reaction. No acknowledgment. Process continued.

Her shoulders slumped.

"But I won't kill you," she said quietly. "Because killing you kills them. And I won't do that. I won't choose purity over people."

The words felt heavy as they left her, settling into her bones.

She lifted her hand, hovering inches from the organism's surface. Heat licked at her skin, familiar now, almost reassuring. Her fingers trembled.

"I'll remember," she said instead. "I'll remember what this cost. Even if no one else does."

She let her hand fall back to her side.

The chamber held its breathless stillness. The organism pulsed on, ancient and unyielding, continuing the work it had never paused to question.

Amara turned away and began the climb back up, boots whispering against the warmed floor, the air pressing close as if it wanted to follow her. Heat clung to her skin long after she left the chamber, a residue she could feel settling deeper than muscle. Each step carried the same steady rhythm she'd felt below, a reminder that the pulse traveled everywhere now, woven into the bones of the place.

She didn't go far.

Halfway up the corridor, she lowered herself to the floor and sat, back against the curved wall, palms resting on her knees. The surface beneath her was warm enough to soften tension, warm enough to invite stillness. She closed her eyes and let time slip.

An hour passed. Maybe two. The lights didn't change. The air didn't cool. Her body didn't protest. She existed there, breathing in sync with something vast and patient, her thoughts slowing until they lost their edges. Anger dulled. Grief loosened its grip. What remained felt quieter, heavier—an acceptance she didn't welcome but couldn't deny.

When she finally stood, her joints moved easily. She sealed the chamber behind her with deliberate care, fingers steady on the panel, the lock engaging with a muted finality. The sound echoed briefly, then dissolved.

Up in the living levels, motion resumed around her without pause.

Footsteps overlapped in the corridors. Voices drifted through open doors. The scent of food traveled on warm currents of air. Children darted between adults, laughter bright and unguarded, their energy spilling freely into spaces carved for survival rather than joy.

The town breathed.

Amara followed the sound of voices into the common area. Tables had been pushed together to make room for activity. A group of adults worked through a stack of supply crates, hands moving in practiced coordination. At the far end, children sat cross-legged on the floor with paper spread between them, crayons scattered like confetti.

Isaac Reed knelt among them, brow furrowed in concentration.

She stopped a few steps away, watching as his hand moved carefully across the page. Lines emerged—clean, deliberate, confident. When he noticed her, his face brightened.

"What are you working on?" she asked, crouching beside him.

He lifted the paper proudly.

It showed the town from the side, layers stacked neatly atop one another. Living spaces. Schools. Greenhouses. At the very bottom, a large red circle filled the page, shaded with care.

"The heart," he said.

Amara studied the drawing. "The heart of what?"

He tilted his head, as if the answer were obvious. "The town. The thing that keeps us warm."

She looked at him. "Everyone knows about it?"

He nodded. "Yeah. We learn about it in class. Just... not like this." He tapped the circle gently. "We don't talk about it much."

"Why?"

Isaac shrugged, picking up a crayon and adding small lines radiating outward from the red shape. "Talking about it makes people feel funny. But it doesn't feel funny to me. It just feels normal."

"Normal," she repeated.

"Like breathing," he said. "You don't talk about breathing all the time. You just do it."

She smiled faintly and sat back on her heels. He returned to his drawing, humming under his breath, completely absorbed. His fingers moved with certainty, mapping tunnels and rooms with a precision that spoke of familiarity rather than curiosity.

Amara watched him, this child shaped by conditions he would never question, whose sense of home extended downward into depths most people would never see. He would grow here. He would love here. His children would be born already suited to this place, their bodies answering warmth and cold in ways the surface world could no longer tolerate.

Continuation, she realized, rarely announced itself as triumph.

It arrived quietly, dressed as routine.

She rose and left the common area, the sound of Isaac's humming following her for a few steps before blending into the general murmur of life. Corridors curved gently around her as she walked, lights reflecting off smooth walls, footsteps softened by resilient flooring.

Her quarters waited at the end of a narrow hall.

The room was small, functional, once a storage space repurposed out of necessity. A cot pressed against one wall. A desk sat beneath a light panel. Shelves lined the opposite side, already crowded with journals and binders, their spines labeled in her neat, careful hand.

Amara stepped inside and closed the door.

The room held steady warmth, a temperature her body accepted without thought. She set her hands on the desk and stood there for a long moment, listening to the muted sounds of the town beyond the walls. Pipes murmured. Air circulated. Somewhere nearby, someone laughed.

She reached for one of the journals and slid it back into place, aligning it carefully with the others.

Witnessing, she thought, did not require distance anymore.

It required memory.

She sat on the cot, back straight, hands folded loosely in her lap, and let herself breathe in time with the place that had claimed her.

On the wall above her desk, the letter waited.

The paper had yellowed slightly at the edges now, curling where the pins pierced it. Her mother's handwriting remained steady and familiar, the ink pressed deep enough to leave faint grooves she could trace with her eyes even without touching it.

Choose with your whole heart.

Amara read the line the way some people touched talismans. Not for comfort. For grounding.

She had chosen. Or something inside her had chosen first, quietly, efficiently, long before her mind was ready to follow. The result was the same. She woke each day in this room. She breathed air warmed from below. She moved through tunnels that never cooled. Her body functioned without protest.

Outside her door, the town lived.

Footsteps passed at regular intervals. Someone laughed—a short burst that bounced down the corridor and dissolved. A cart rattled by, wheels humming softly over the floor. The scent of food drifted through the ventilation system, rich and sustaining, grown in light that never flickered and soil that never froze.

Grayhaven had settled into itself.

Children raced past one another in the common spaces, cheeks flushed, voices bright. Adults spoke in low, practical tones, conversations shaped by schedules and supply lists and sleeping rotations. Hands were busy. Bodies were fed. Systems held.

The greenhouses pushed out leaves and fruit in steady abundance. The water stayed warm. The power never faltered. The tunnels breathed heat upward without effort, without pause.

Seventy feet above them, the world ended.

Amara pictured it sometimes—not as it was, but as it must be now. Snow piled beyond scale. Wind scouring everything down to shape and pressure. Temperatures so low that even motion failed. A surface no longer meant for footprints or shelter or skin.

A place that might as well have been another planet.

The thought didn't frighten her the way it once had. It sat somewhere dull and distant, like a memory borrowed from someone else's life. Her body didn't react. Her pulse didn't change. The cold outside no longer registered as threat so much as irrelevance.

The town endured.

Changed. Integrated. Quietly reshaped into something that functioned where its ancestors could not.

Alive.

She rolled her chair back from the desk and stood, crossing the small room in three steps. The cot creaked faintly as she sat, the sound oddly loud in the steady hush. She leaned her elbows on her knees and let her hands hang loose, fingers relaxed, warm.

Alive.

The word felt heavier than it should.

In a world where entire regions were failing, where temperatures dropped without regard for borders or history, survival had become currency. Proof. Permission. The town had paid the price and received its reward.

Was that morality?

Or was morality another luxury that only existed while conditions allowed it?

Amara didn't have an answer. The question slid away every time she reached for it, dissolving into something more immediate: breath in, breath out, warmth held, work to be done.

She turned back to the desk and opened a fresh notebook.

The paper whispered softly beneath her pen. Ink flowed clean and dark. Dates no longer mattered much, but she wrote them anyway. Recorded temperatures that no one felt anymore. Logged births and deaths that balanced themselves with eerie precision. Sketched diagrams of tunnel expansions and agricultural yields and physiological changes that no longer surprised her.

She wrote because writing slowed time.

Because it fixed moments in place when everything else insisted on moving forward.

She wrote for her mother, whose refusal had ended in cold and silence. She wrote for herself, so that some version of her would remain legible even as her body changed the terms of what survival required.

Outside the room, someone knocked on a door and waited. Somewhere farther away, a child cried briefly, then stopped. Life corrected itself quickly here.

Amara kept writing.

She wrote about the warmth. About the quiet. About the way no one looked up anymore, because there was nothing above them that could answer back.

She wrote about the last time choices had felt clean.

About when being human had meant more than persistence.

Someone had to remember that version of the world.

Even if no one asked for it.

Even if the town had already moved on.

Even if the only victory left was the simple, relentless act of continuing.

She opened a fresh journal and rested it on the desk, the spine creaking softly as if it had already been used before. The paper inside was bright, almost luminous under the warm overhead light. Too clean. Too hopeful. She pressed her palm flat against the first page, feeling the faint vibration traveling through the wood, through the wall, through her bones.

The pulse below never stopped.

She picked up her pen.

Ink touched paper.

*What we became was shaped by forces older than fear or choice. What we had to become was the price of continuing to breathe when the world turned hostile. Survival demanded its cost, paid slowly, quietly, and without the option of refusal.*

The words came slower after that. Each line required weight behind it. She wrote through the subtle rise and fall beneath her feet, through the warmth that pressed upward without mercy or malice, through the awareness that the thing below had already moved beyond this town, beyond these people, beyond her.

It planned for scale.

She could feel that now.

The organism continued its work with the patience of geology and the certainty of mathematics. Heat drawn inward. Energy redistributed. Systems adjusted. Thresholds recalculated again and again, always pointing toward colder futures. The kind of cold that erased oceans. The kind that cracked atmospheres open. The kind that left only two outcomes: adaptation or absence.

Her hand tightened around the pen.

*We are still alive. Changed. Adapted. Dependent. But alive.*

The surface world remained distant in her thoughts, a pale memory of light and wind and exposure. Whatever still existed up there lived on borrowed time. She sensed that the organism understood this with brutal clarity. It had not awakened for Grayhaven alone. The town had been a test site. A proof of concept. A rehearsal.

*When the real event arrived, there would be no time for debate.*

*No warnings.*

*Only thresholds.*

She paused, staring at the words she had written, then continued.

*The surface has no idea what waits beneath it. Maybe that is mercy. Maybe understanding only ever comes after it is useless.*

Her chest tightened. A familiar ache spread behind her ribs, sharp enough to make her pause, dull enough to endure. She breathed through it, matching her rhythm to the slow cadence rising from the depths. Her heart answered easily.

That truth settled fully now, heavy and unavoidable. She had chased alternatives until the ground itself rejected her. She had stood at the edge of escape and felt her body revolt. She had reached for warnings and watched them dissolve in disbelief and bureaucracy and fear.

Every path had closed with the same quiet finality.

She wrote again.

*Survival does not ask permission. Change does not wait for agreement. The future selects what can remain.*

Her pen hovered.

She swallowed.

*I wanted another ending.*

The sentence wavered, ink darkening where her hand trembled. She steadied herself and finished the thought.

*I could not find one.*

The warmth beneath her pressed upward, steady as breath. It wrapped around her spine, her limbs, the base of her skull. She felt it in her teeth. In her palms. In the soft center of her chest where instinct lived.

She continued writing because stopping felt like surrender.

*We are the changed. We are what comes next. And I am still here to witness it.*

Her eyes burned. She blinked hard and kept going, the page blurring, then clearing again as moisture froze briefly at her lashes before melting away.

*I will remember what we were. I will record what we became. So that if the cold ever loosens its grip—if the surface ever opens again—someone will understand the price.*

*Even if that someone is only me.*

The pen slowed. The page filled. Her hand ached.

She closed the journal.

The sound landed softly in the small room, absorbed by walls that had learned to hold heat and silence in equal measure. She leaned back in the chair and let her gaze wander. The cot. The shelves heavy with records. The pinned letter above the desk, edges curled, words worn thin by repetition.

This space held everything she had left.

It held *her*.

She stood and crossed the room, bare feet warm against the floor. She touched the wall once, just above where the vibration felt strongest. The pulse answered immediately, firm and present, a reassurance offered without intention.

This was home now.

A shelter carved into inevitability.

She understood, with a clarity that hurt more than confusion ever had, that she would make peace with this place—or she would learn to live alongside the absence of it. Either way, her body had already chosen persistence.

Grayhaven endured, through deepening cold. Through forced change. Through the quiet shedding of old definitions. It endured because endurance was the only currency left.

Her survival carried no pride. No triumph. Only continuation.

She reached up and turned off the light.

Darkness folded around the room, complete and intimate. The warmth remained. The pulse below remained. She lay down on the cot and pulled the thin blanket over herself out of habit rather than need.

Her heartbeat slowed.

Then aligned.

She listened to the rhythm beneath the floor, beneath the rock, beneath the world that had once been open sky. The line between her body and the organism blurred until it felt irrelevant, until she could no longer tell where one ended and the other began.

Fear rose, sharp and unmistakable.

Fear meant she still remembered.

Above her, snow continued to fall into a world that could no longer receive it. Below her, something ancient and prepared continued shaping the survivors it would carry forward.

And in between, Amara lay awake, breathing in time with a future that would outlast everything she had once called human.

The first change arrived as pressure.

The air tightened around her chest, subtle but unmistakable, as though the space itself had drawn closer. Her body adjusted immediately. Her breath slowed, deepened, settled into a rhythm that felt deliberate rather than automatic. Her ribs expanded fully, easily, as if they had been waiting for this moment.

The pulse beneath the floor shifted.

It sank deeper, broadened, filled the structure with a steadier cadence. Warmth rose in a controlled wave, enough to prickle along her skin, enough that the blanket became irrelevant. She pushed it aside and lay flat, palms against the mattress, spine aligned with the vibration threading through the building.

The lights in the corridor flickered once.

Then stabilized.

Far above—so distant it felt abstract—the surface crossed a breaking point.

She sensed it the way bodies sense altitude before sight catches up. A collapse unfolding without spectacle. Systems unraveling all at once. A cascade that carried finality without noise.

Her stomach tightened.

Anticipation spread through her instead of fear.

The walls responded first. A faint contraction ran through them, structural tolerances recalibrating in real time. The floor warmed again, unmistakably now. Heat rolled upward with intent, wrapping the living levels in protection that felt ancient and practiced.

Emergency systems shifted without announcement.

Doors sealed. Airflow redirected. Power redistributed. The town moved as one body, unstartled, prepared.

Amara sat up.

Her heart beat strong and even, utterly unconcerned.

She stood and placed her bare feet on the floor. Warmth met her instantly, intimate and grounding. Her balance felt flawless. Her vision sharpened, contrast deepening, edges clarifying as though her eyes had learned a better way to see.

She opened the door.

People stood in the corridor, emerging quietly, faces composed. Parents drew children close with practiced calm. Someone laughed once—short, breathless, relieved.

A woman from the greenhouse met Amara's gaze and nodded.

"It's starting," she said.

Amara nodded back.

"Yes."

They all felt it now.

The organism extended inward, drawing heat from depths humanity had never reached, redistributing energy with flawless efficiency. Warmth intensified in precise increments, calibrated to bodies already shaped to receive it.

Above them, the surface surrendered.

Temperatures plunged beyond tolerance. Materials failed. Storm systems collapsed into sustained violence. The last balances humanity had relied on gave way.

Amara returned to her room and closed the door, not to retreat, but to witness. She sat on the cot, hands resting loosely on her thighs. Her body thrummed now, every system aligned, every signal clean.

The warmth no longer felt external.

It bloomed from within.

Recognition swept through her as something final settled into place. Pressure behind her eyes dissolved. Her breathing deepened again, lungs expanding with effortless efficiency. Blood moved with purpose, no wasted motion, no excess.

Her skin flushed, cooled, then stabilized into perfect equilibrium.

A soft laugh escaped her. It surprised her—not because it felt wrong, but because it felt earned. "So, this is it," she whispered.

The pulse answered by synchronizing completely. Her heartbeat adjusted until distinction disappeared. She pressed her palm to her chest and felt a single, unified rhythm.

Memory surfaced.

Her mother. The bench. Frozen tears.

"I'm sorry," Amara said, though the words carried no weight here.

The apology drifted away, unneeded.

She turned off the light again. Darkness filled the room—dense, warm, alive with sensation. The walls glowed faintly with retained heat. The floor vibrated with certainty.

Above them, the last fragile systems failed.

Below them, something ancient completed its preparation.

Amara lay back and closed her eyes. The cold beyond the rock no longer mattered. It could erase the surface entirely.

She would not feel it.

Her breath slowed until it matched the pulse exactly. Thought thinned into focus. This was the beginning.

The dark closed in and did not retreat, settling into place with a weight that felt final, as if the world itself had exhaled and gone still, leaving nothing beyond it to wait or return. Within that stillness, Amara smiled—a small, private curve of her mouth, steady and unafraid—as the future closed around her and the last traces of the unadapted world faded into silence.

Somewhere far above, buried under ice and distance and histories that no longer had witnesses, the world that shaped her disappeared without ceremony. Down here, warmth endured, bodies endured, memory endured—thin, stubborn, human in the only way it could be now. Amara lay still in the dark, breathing with the pulse beneath the ground, knowing she had chosen survival the same way everyone eventually did, by staying. If anyone were left to look back, to wonder where humanity had gone and why it never returned, she imagined the thought drifting through the cold like a message carved into ice: *Wish You Were Here.*

# Stay Connected

Hey there, amazing reader!

I hope you enjoyed diving into my world of stories as much as I loved creating them! Your thoughts and feedback mean everything to me, and I'd love to hear what you think. Whether it's a review, a favorite quote, or just a quick "OMG, I need more!"—I'm all ears!

**Your Reviews Matter!** If you loved what you just read (or even if you have thoughts on how it made you feel), leaving a review helps more readers discover my books. Plus, it totally makes my day!

Let's stay connected! Follow me, tag me, and send me a message—I love chatting with fellow book lovers!

**Blog:** MyuniqueGreen.com
**Instagram: @_cmajor_**
**Snapchat:** Cece_major

Can't wait to hear from you! Until next time—Keep turning those pages!

# About Myunique

Myunique C. Green is an award-winning independent author and the founder of iWriteBooks Publishing. Known for her dynamic range, she writes psychological thrillers, Southern Gothic, fantasy, YA, romance, and more—always centering Black women and crafting stories that blend emotional depth with bold, imaginative storytelling. Her books have been featured in book clubs, libraries, and literary spaces across the country, supported by a dedicated readership and a rapidly expanding catalog.

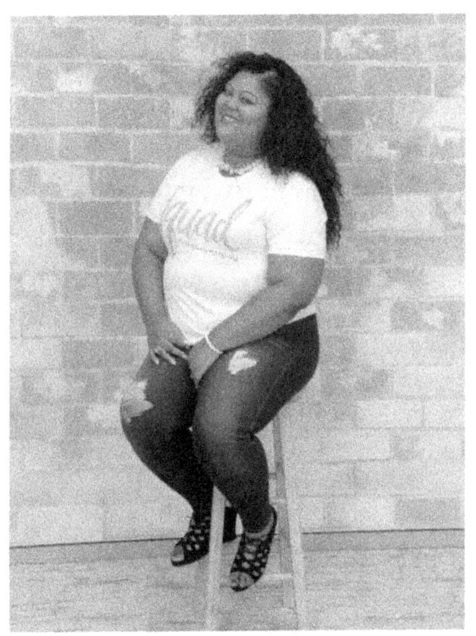

Alongside her writing career, Myunique is a special education teacher, a mother, and a creative entrepreneur who produces multimedia projects, and original artwork that complement her stories. Her work is grounded in intention, community, and craft, and she continues to build new worlds that resonate with readers seeking powerful, character-driven fiction.

Excerpt From

# The Second Death

The fluorescent hum of the hospital lights burned into Brintis Downs' skull, sharp and sterile, washing everything in a sickly yellow hue. The glass between him and Terrica might as well have been a wall, thick and unbreakable, sealing her in as she convulsed on the hospital bed.

Her body jerked violently, her back arching, fingers clawing at the thin blanket as if she were trying to escape her own skin. The restraints on her wrists rattled against the bed frame. Foam bubbled at the corners of her lips. The monitors behind her screamed in protest—erratic beeps, warnings no one in the room seemed able to do anything about.

Brintis' breath caught. He slammed his palm against the glass. "Do something!"

No one turned.

A nurse stood by the IV, her fingers gripping the pole so tightly her knuckles went white. A doctor in a full hazmat suit barked orders to the others, his voice muffled behind the mask. A second nurse—a young man barely out of school, judging by the way his hands trembled—tried to steady Terrica's arm, but her body bucked, nearly throwing him back.

Brintis felt useless. No, worse than useless. He felt like a goddamn spectator at the end of the world.

The hallway behind him stank of bleach and sweat. Hospitals had always smelled like death, but this was different. This was *new*. The whole floor buzzed with an energy that felt just shy of hysteria—doctors moving too quickly, nurses whispering to each other in hushed, frantic tones. Past the glass, past the chaos of Terrica's failing body, Brintis caught a glimpse of another room across the hall.

A woman lay on a cot, motionless.

A white sheet had already been pulled over her face.

Brintis' stomach dropped.

"Sir," a voice called to him. "Step away from the glass."

He turned to find a security guard standing a few feet away, a hand resting on the baton at his hip. A gun, too. Brintis wasn't sure if it was meant for him or what was on the other side of the glass.

"Like hell," he spat. "That's my *wife*."

"She's infected." The guard's face was unreadable, but his voice carried the same dull detachment Brintis had heard from every other official since the moment Terrica was admitted. "She's in the late stage."

Late stage.

Brintis didn't know what that meant. No one did, not really. They had been using words like *progression* and *deterioration*, throwing them around like they knew what the hell was happening. Like the *Ashwood Virus* was just another flu strain, something predictable, something solvable.

But there was nothing predictable about the way people were dying.

Or worse, *not* dying.

"Terrica," he whispered, pressing his forehead against the glass.

Her eyes snapped open.

Brintis recoiled.

They weren't *hers*. Not really. Not anymore.

Her pupils had dilated into black pools, the irises barely visible, clouded like stormwater. Her gaze darted, unfocused, her lips parting as she tried to speak. A low, wet sound gurgled in her throat.

Brintis slammed his fist against the barrier. "Hold on, baby. Just—just hold on."

She *heard* him. He knew she did. Because for a flicker of a second, the frantic, unseeing stare locked onto him. Recognition flared in the depths of her gaze. A flicker of *Terrica*, drowning in whatever fever was eating her alive.

Then she started *screaming*.

A wretched, bone-deep sound that cut through the walls, through the glass, through *him*.

The doctor grabbed a syringe. One of the nurses pinned her down. The young man who had tried to steady her arm turned away, his shoulders heaving.

The security guard took a step forward, his hand tightening on the baton.

The screaming stopped.

Brintis blinked.

Terrica lay still, her body twisted at an unnatural angle, chest barely rising. The doctor leaned over her, shining a light into her unresponsive eyes. The monitors behind her flattened into a long, unwavering beep.

No one moved.

Brintis took a step back from the glass, his heart pounding so hard it drowned out everything else. The guard sighed. The doctor straightened. A nurse reached for a sheet.

Brintis pressed his hand against the glass one last time, fingers splayed, waiting—*praying*—for Terrica to open her eyes again.

Because if she did…

He wasn't sure if he wanted it to be a miracle.

Or a warning.

Brintis didn't realize he was still holding his breath until the doctor peeled off his gloves and said, "Time of death: 2:37 AM."

His knees nearly buckled.

The words should have meant something—should have hit like a hammer, driving reality straight through his chest—but all he felt was numb. Like his brain had locked him out of his own body, shielding him from the weight of it all.

Terrica was dead.

Again.

Brintis pressed his fist against his mouth, his breath coming in short, uneven bursts. His skin felt too tight, his pulse too loud.

She had just been screaming. Just been looking at him. There was no way she could be *gone* that fast.

Someone touched his shoulder. He flinched.

The doctor stood beside him, still suited up in full protective gear, his face hidden behind the plastic shield of his hazmat helmet. His voice, though, was clinical, practiced.

"Mr. Downs. I need to prepare you for next steps."

Brintis barely heard him. His eyes were locked on Terrica's still form. The way they were already pulling a sheet over her, as if she weren't even a person anymore. Just *a risk to manage*.

He snapped his head toward the doctor, voice hoarse. "Is she gonna turn?"

A pause.

Brintis saw it—the brief hesitation, the flicker of uncertainty before the man answered.

"No," the doctor said. "She hadn't progressed enough."

It should have been a relief. It wasn't.

Brintis let out a shuddering breath. "So that's it?" He gestured at the lifeless form of his wife. "She's just—*gone*?"

"Yes. But." Another pause. The doctor cleared his throat. "The virus can be… unpredictable. A wild card, if you will. Some patients have exhibited post-mortem reanimation at stages we didn't expect. Which is why we recommend immediate cremation."

Brintis' stomach twisted. "Cremation?"

The doctor nodded. "The hospital handles it for free. Quick and effective. We take no risks."

The words landed like an anvil to the chest.

Brintis looked back at Terrica, her body so still under the sheet. The hands that had once held his face, traced lazy circles against his wrist while they lay in bed, now covered—hidden—like they had never mattered.

They wanted to burn her. Reduce her to *ash* like she had never existed.

Like she hadn't just fought for every last breath.

Like she wasn't *his wife.*

Brintis' fingers curled into fists. "No."

The doctor exhaled. "Mr. Downs, I understand this is difficult, but it's the safest—"

"I said no."

The security guard from earlier took a half-step forward, as if preparing to intervene. Brintis ignored him. His whole body felt like it was vibrating, the air in his lungs thick with rage and disbelief.

"She's gone," Brintis said, his voice shaking. "But she's still Terrica. And I'm not letting you burn her like some damn biohazard."

He didn't know what the hell he was going to do next. But he knew one thing: *Terrica wasn't leaving this world as ashes in a government-run furnace.*

Not his wife.

Never.

The nurse beside the doctor glanced away, pressing her lips together like she didn't want to be in this conversation.

The doctor kept his voice even. "The virus doesn't always follow the rules. The safest course of action is immediate cremation."

Brintis' body went rigid. "No."

"Mr. Downs—"

"I said no." His voice had an edge to it now, sharp enough to slice through the sterile air.

The doctor exhaled. "Mr. Downs, we're offering the hospital's cremation services free of charge. It's the most effective way to ensure there are no… complications."

"Complications?" Brintis let out a hollow laugh, shaking his head. "Listen to yourself. You're talking about her like she's an *it*. Like she's already gone."

"She *is*." The words landed like a gut punch. The doctor softened, but his tone remained firm. "The virus is unpredictable. We've lost good people because they hesitated. I've seen families lose their loved ones twice. I wouldn't suggest this if it weren't necessary."

Brintis' jaw locked. His heartbeat thundered in his ears.

Twice.

The word hit him in a way he wasn't ready for.

There were whispers about it. News reports that were swiftly pulled, rumors floating around online. People who had died *once* only to come back *wrong*. But that was the late-stage cases, the ones who had already gone rabid before their bodies shut down. That wasn't Terrica.

She had been sick, yeah. Feverish. Confused. But she had still been *her*. Now they wanted him to agree to this like she was nothing more than a liability?

His hands clenched at his sides. “I’m taking her home.”

The nurse sucked in a quiet breath. The doctor’s expression didn’t change.

“That’s not advisable.”

Brintis set his jaw. “Don’t care.”

Silence stretched between them.

Then, finally, the doctor relented. “If that’s your choice, we won’t force you.”

The doctor peeled off his gloves, tossing them into the biohazard bin. “We’ll handle the paperwork. But Mr. Downs—” He hesitated, then leveled Brintis with a look that wasn’t *just* clinical detachment anymore. There was something else there. Something *warning*. “If she comes back… don’t hesitate.”

Brintis didn’t answer. He just turned back toward the glass, toward the woman who had been his whole world.

She wasn’t coming back.

She couldn’t.

Because if she did…

He wasn’t sure he’d be able to do what needed to be done.

The hours after that thought passed in a blur of small, brutal tasks. Paperwork spread across the kitchen table, forms stamped and signed with hands that didn’t feel like his. Names, dates, boxes to check. Terrica reduced to lines of ink and a cause of death that felt obscene in its neatness. The pen slipped once, leaving a dark scratch across the page, and Brintis stared at it longer than necessary, breathing through the tightness in his chest.

The apartment smelled faintly of disinfectant and cold coffee. He hadn’t opened a window since the hospital. Every room felt frozen in the moment she’d left it—her jacket draped over the chair, one shoe kicked halfway under the couch, the faint impression of her body still pressed into the mattress. Each object carried weight. Each one asked a question he couldn’t answer.

Sleep came in fragments. When it did, it dragged him back to the hospital bed, the restraints, the sound of her voice breaking into something animal and unfamiliar. He woke with his jaw clenched so hard it ached, his throat raw from swallowing back sounds he refused to let out.

The mortuary call was worse than the hospital. The man on the other end spoke softly, respectfully, as if kindness could soften the fact that they were discussing a body. Options were offered. Materials. Timelines. Brintis answered automatically, agreeing to the simplest version of everything because anything more felt like an indulgence he didn't deserve. He hung up and stood in the kitchen afterward, phone still in his hand, trying to remember when his life had narrowed to decisions like this.

Terrica's mother called once. He let it ring. Later, she texted. A single line asking when. He stared at the screen until it dimmed, then placed the phone face-down on the counter like it might accuse him if he looked at it too long.

The day before the service, he laid out clothes he wouldn't remember choosing. Black fabric pooled across the bed. It smelled like storage and unfamiliar detergent. He pressed his face into Terrica's sweater for just a second longer than he should have, breathing her in until the ache sharpened, until his eyes burned. He folded it carefully and put it back. Some things felt too much like a goodbye.

By the time the morning came, he felt hollowed out. Like the worst of the pain had already passed through him and left nothing solid behind. The world looked muted, colors washed thin by overcast light. Sounds arrived dulled, as if wrapped in cotton. Even his own footsteps felt distant, belonging to someone else moving his body through space.

The funeral was quiet.

Too quiet.

Brintis had expected more people. Terrica had friends—colleagues from the marketing firm where she'd worked before the outbreak, neighbors she'd chatted with over coffee, college friends who still checked in every now and then. But the Ashwood Virus had changed the rules of mourning.

No one wanted to stand too close to grief anymore. Not when grief could be contagious.

The cemetery was nearly empty. Just Brintis, the funeral director, and Terrica's mother, Claudia, who stood a few feet away, her face hidden behind a black veil. She hadn't spoken to him since the hospital. Hadn't looked at him, either.

Brintis didn't blame her.

He'd made the choice to bring Terrica home that first night, to keep her in their bed instead of letting the hospital take her. Claudia had called it reckless. Selfish. She'd screamed at him through the phone, her voice raw with terror and rage.

"What if she turns? What if she comes back and you can't—"

He'd hung up on her.

Because she didn't understand. Terrica was gone. Really gone. The virus hadn't taken her far enough to bring her back. The doctors had said so. The tests had confirmed it.

She wasn't coming back.

The coffin was simple. Pine, unvarnished, with brass handles that gleamed dully in the overcast afternoon light. Brintis had picked it himself. No flowers. No frills. Just a box to hold what was left of the woman he loved.

The funeral director cleared his throat. "Mr. Downs, would you like to say a few words?"

Brintis shook his head.

What the hell was he supposed to say? That Terrica had been everything? That she'd made him laugh when the world felt too heavy, that she'd believed in him when he didn't believe in himself? That she'd died screaming, her body convulsing as the fever burned through her brain?

Words felt useless.

The director nodded, signaling to the workers waiting by the grave. They moved forward, lowering the coffin into the earth with mechanical precision.

Claudia let out a choked sob.

Brintis stood still, his hands buried in his pockets, his chest hollow.

The dirt hit the coffin with a dull thud. Then another. And another.

He didn't move until it was over. Until Terrica was buried six feet under, sealed away from the world that had killed her.

Claudia left without a word.

Brintis stayed.

He stood there as the sun dipped lower, as the shadows stretched long across the gravestones, as the workers packed up their tools and drove away.

He stood there until he couldn't feel his legs anymore.

Finally, he walked away. Because that's what you did when someone died.

You buried them, and you moved on.

www.ingramcontent.com/pod-product-compliance
Lightning Source LLC
LaVergne TN
LVHW020658110826
845149LV00012B/2031

* 9 7 8 1 1 0 5 6 2 7 6 2 0 *